...three hands shot for their hips

No stop-watch could have caught the differing lengths of time which each required for the draw. The muzzle of Hurley's revolver was not clear of the holster—the gun of Diaz was nearly at the level when Pierre's weapon exploded at his hip. The bullet cut through the wrist of Hurley. Never again would that slender, supple hand fly over the cards, doing things other than they seemed. He made no effort to escape from the next bullet, but stood looking down at his broken wrist; horror for the moment gave a dignity oddly out of place with his usual appearance. He alone in all the room was moveless.

The crowd, undecided for an instant, broke for the doors at the first shot; Pierre le Rouge pitched to the floor as Diaz leaped forward, the revolver in either hand spitting lead and fire...

RIDERS OF
THE SILENCES

RIDERS OF
THE SILENCES

B

BERKLEY BOOKS, NEW YORK

Originally published in *Argosy* in 1919 under the title *Luck*, written under the pseudonym of John Frederick, and first published in book form by the H. K. Fly Company in 1920 under the title *Riders of the Silences*.

This Berkley book contains the complete
text of the original hardcover edition.

RIDERS OF THE SILENCES

A Berkley Book / published by arrangement with
Dodd, Mead & Company

PRINTING HISTORY
Dodd, Mead edition / August 1986
Berkley edition / October 1987

ISBN: 0-425-10346-3

A BERKLEY BOOK ® TM 757,375
Berkley Books are published by The Berkley Publishing Group,
200 Madison Avenue, New York, NY 10016.
The name "BERKLEY" and the "B" logo
are trademarks belonging to Berkley Publishing Corporation.

PRINTED IN THE UNITED STATES OF AMERICA

10   9   8   7   6   5   4   3   2   1

Prologue

The Great West, prior to the century's turn, abounded in legend. Stories were told of fabled gunmen whose bullets always magically found their mark, of mighty stallions whose tireless gallop rivaled the speed of the wind, of glorious women whose beauty stunned mind and heart. But nowhere in the vast spread of the mountain-desert country was there a greater legend told than the story of Red Pierre and the phantom gunfighter, McGurk.

These two men of the wilderness, so unalike, of widely-differing backgrounds, had in common a single trait: each was unbeatable. Fate brought them clashing together, thunder to thunder, lightning to lightning. They were destined to meet at the crossroads of a long, long trail . . . a trail which began in the northern wastes of Canada and led, finally, to a deadly confrontation in the mountains of the Far West.

RIDERS OF
THE SILENCES

1

It seemed that Father Anthony gathered all the warmth of the short northern summer and kept it for winter use, for his good nature was an actual physical force. From his ruddy face beamed such a kindliness that people reached out toward him as they might extend their hands toward a comfortable fire.

All the labors of his work as an inspector of Jesuit institutions across the length and breadth of Canada could not lessen the good father's enthusiasm; his smile was as indefatigable as his critical eyes. The one looked sharply into every corner of a room and every nook and hidden cranny of thoughts and deeds; the other veiled the criticism and soothed the wounds of vanity.

On this day, however, the sharp eyes grew a little less keen and somewhat wider, while that smile was fixed rather by habit than inclination. In fact, his expression might be called a frozen kindliness as he looked across the table to Father Victor.

It required a most indomitable geniality, indeed, to outface the rigid piety of Jean Paul Victor. His missionary work had carried him far north, where the cold burns men thin. The zeal which drove him north and north and north over untracked regions, drove him until his body failed, drove him even now, though his body was crippled.

A mighty yearning, and a still mightier self-contempt whipped him on, and the school over which he was master groaned and suffered under his régime.

Father Anthony said gently: "Are there none among all your lads, dear Father Victor, whom you find something more than imperfect machines?"

The man of the north drew from a pocket of his robe a letter. His lean fingers touched it almost with a caress.

"One. Pierre Ryder. He shall carry on my mission in the north. I, who am silent, have done much; but Pierre will do more. I had to fight my first battle to conquer my own stubborn soul, and the battle left me weak for the great work in the snows, but Pierre will not fight that battle, for I have trained him.

"This letter is for him. Shall we not carry it to him? For two days I have not seen Pierre."

Father Anthony winced.

He said: "Do you deny yourself even the pleasure of the lad's company? Alas, Father Victor, you forge your own spurs and goad yourself with your own hands. What harm is there in being often with the lad?"

The sneer returned to the lips of Jean Paul Victor.

"The purpose would be lost—lost to my eyes and lost to his—the purpose for which I have lived and for which he shall live. When I first saw him he was a child, a baby, but he came to me and took one finger of my hand in his small fist and looked up to me. Ah, Gabrielle, the smile of an infant goes to the heart swifter than the thrust of a knife! I looked down upon him and I knew that I was chosen to teach the child. There was a voice that spoke in me. You will smile, but even now I think I can hear it."

"I swear to you that I believe," said Father Anthony.

"Another man would have given Pierre a Bible and a Latin grammar and a cell. I gave him the testament and the grammar; I gave him also the wild north country to say his prayers in and patter his Latin. I taught his mind, but I did not forget his body.

"He is to go out among wild men. He must have strength

of the spirit. He must also have a strength of the body that they will understand and respect. He can ride a horse standing; he can run a hundred miles in a day behind a dog-team. He can wrestle and fight with his hands, for skilled men have taught him. I have made him a thunder-bolt to hurl among the ignorant and the unenlightened; and this is the hand which shall wield it. Ha!

"It is now hardly a six month since he saved a trapper from a bobcat and killed the animal with a knife. It must have been my prayers which saved him from the teeth and the claws."

Good Father Anthony rose.

"You have described a young David. I am eager to see him. Let us go."

Father Victor nodded, and the two went out together. The chill of the open was hardly more than the bitter cold inside the building, but there was a wind that drove the cold through the blood and bones of a man.

They staggered along against it until they came to a small house, long and low. On the sheltered side they paused to take breath, and Father Victor explained: "This is his hour in the gymnasium. To make the body strong required thought and care. Mere riding and running and swinging of the ax will not develop every muscle. Here Pierre works every day. His teachers of boxing and wres-tling have abandoned him."

There was almost a smile on the lean face.

"The last man left with a swollen jaw and limping on one leg."

Here he opened the door, and they slipped inside. The air was warmed by a big stove, and the room—for the afternoon was dark—lighted by two swinging lanterns sus-pended from the low roof. By that illumination Father Anthony saw two men stripped naked, save for a loin-cloth, and circling each other slowly in the center of a ring

3

which was fenced in with ropes and floored with a padded mat.

Of the two wrestlers, one was a veritable giant, swarthy of skin, hairy-chested. His great hands were extended to grasp or to parry—his head lowered with a ferocious scowl—and across his forehead swayed a tuft of black, shaggy hair. He might have stood for one of those northern barbarians whom the Romans loved to pit against their native champions in the arena. He was the greater because of the opponent he faced, and it was upon this opponent that the eyes of Father Anthony centered.

Like Father Victor, he was caught first by the bright hair. It was a dark red, and where the light struck it strongly there were places like fire. Down from this hair the light slipped like running water over a lithe body, slender at the hips, strong-chested, round and smooth of limb, with long muscles leaping and trembling at every move.

He, like the big fighter, circled cautiously about, but the impression he gave was as different from the other as day is from night. His head was carried high; in place of a scowl, he smiled with a sort of eagerness, a light which was partly exultation and partly mischief sparkled in his eyes. Once or twice the giant caught at the other, but David slipped from under the grip of Goliath easily. It seemed as if his skin were oiled. The big man snarled with anger, and lunged more eagerly at Pierre.

The two, abandoning their feints, suddenly rushed together, and the swarthy arms of the monster slipped around the white body of Pierre. For a moment they whirled, twisting and struggling.

"Now!" murmured Father Victor; and as if in answer to a command, Pierre slipped down, whipped his hands to a new grip, and the two crashed to the mat, with Pierre above.

"Open your eyes, Father Anthony. The lad is safe. How Goliath grunts!"

4

The boy had not cared to follow his advantage, but rose and danced away, laughing softly. The Canuck floundered up and rushed like a furious bull. His downfall was only the swifter. The impact of the two bodies sounded like hands clapped together, and then Goliath rose into the air, struggling mightily, and pitched with a thud to the mat.

He writhed there, for the wind was knocked from his body by the fall. At length he struggled to a sitting posture and glared up at the conqueror. The boy reached out a hand to his fallen foe.

"You would have thrown me that way the first time," he said, "but you let me change grips on you. In another week you will be too much for me, *bon ami.*"

The other accepted the hand after an instant of hesitation and was dragged to his feet. He stood looking down into the boy's face with a singular grin. But there was no triumph in the eye of Pierre—only a good-natured interest.

"In another week," answered the giant, "there would not be a sound bone in my body."

2

"You have seen him," murmured the tall priest. "Now let us go back and wait for him. I will leave word."

He touched one of the two or three men who were watching the athletes, and whispered his message in the other's ear. Then he went back with Father Anthony.

"You have seen him," he repeated, when they sat once more in the cheerless room. "Now pronounce on him."

The other answered: "I have seen a wonderful body—but the mind, Father Victor?"

"It is as simple as that of a child—his thoughts run as clear as spring water."

"But suppose a strange thought came in the mind of your Pierre. It would be like the pebbles in swift-running spring water. He would carry it on, rushing. It would tear away the old boundaries of his mind—it might wipe out the banks you have set down for him—it might tear away the choicest teachings."

Father Victor sat straight and stiff with stern, set lips. He said dryly: "Father Anthony has been much in the world."

"I speak from the best intention, good father. Look you, now, I have seen that same red hair and those same lighted blue eyes before, and wherever I have seen them has been war and trouble and unrest. I have seen that same smile which stirs the heart of a woman and makes a man reach for his revolver. This boy whose mind is so clear—arm him with a single wrong thought, with a single doubt of the eternal goodness of God's plans, and he will be a thunderbolt indeed, dear Father, but one which even your strong hand could not control."

"I have heard you," said the priest; "but you will see. He is coming now."

There was a knock at the door; then it opened and showed a modest novice in a simple gown of black serge girt at the waist with the flat encircling band. His head was downward; it was not till the blue eyes flashed inquisitively up that Father Anthony recognized Pierre.

The hard voice of Jean Paul Victor pronounced: "This is that Father Anthony of whom I have spoken."

The novice slipped to his knees and folded his hands, while the plump fingers of Father Anthony poised over that dark red hair, pressed smooth on top where the skull-cap rested. The blessing which he spoke was Latin, and Father Victor looked somewhat anxiously toward his protégé till the latter answered in a diction so pure that Cicero himself would have smiled to hear it.

"Stand up!" cried Father Anthony. "By heavens, Jean Paul, it is the purest Latin I have heard this twelvemonth."

And the lad answered: "It must be pure Latin; Father Victor has taught me."

Gabrielle Anthony stared, and to save him from too obvious confusion the other priest interrupted: "I have a letter for you, my son."

And he passed the envelope to Pierre. The latter examined it with interest. "This comes from the south. It is marked from the United States."

"So far!" exclaimed the tall priest. "Give me the letter, lad."

But here he caught the whimsical eyes of Father Anthony, and he allowed his outstretched hand to fall. Yet he scowled as he said: "No; keep it and read it, Pierre."

"I have no great wish to keep it," answered Pierre, studying anxiously the dark brow of the priest.

"It is yours. Open it and read."

The lad obeyed instantly. He shook out the folded paper and moved a little nearer the light. Then he read aloud, as if it had never entered his mind that what was addressed to him might be meant for his eyes alone.

"Morgantown,
"R. F. D. No. 4.

"Son Pierre:

"Here I lie with a chunk of lead from the gun of Bob McGurk resting somewhere in the insides of me, and there ain't no way of doubting that I'm about to go out. Now, I ain't complaining none. I've had my fling. I've eat my meat to order, well done and

7

rare—mostly rare. Maybe some folks will be saying that I've got what I've been asking for, and I know that Bob McGurk got me fair and square, shooting from the hip. That don't help me none, lying here with a through ticket to some place that's farther south than Texas.

"Hell ain't none too bad for me, I know. I ain't whinning none. I just lie here and watch the world getting dimmer until I begin to be seeing things out of my past. That shows the devil ain't losing no time with me. But the thing that comes back oftenest and hits me the hardest is the sight of your mother, lying with you in the hollow of her arm and looking up at me and whispering, 'Dad,' just before she went out."

The hand of the boy fell, and his eyes sought the face of Father Victor. The latter was standing.

"You told me I had no father—"

An imperious arm stretched toward him.

"Give me the letter."

He moved to obey, and then checked himself.

"This is my father's writing, is it not?"

"No, no! It's a lie, Pierre!"

But Pierre stood with the letter held behind his back, and the first doubt in his life stood up darkly in his eyes. Father Victor sank slowly back into his chair, his gaunt frame trembling.

"Read on," he commanded.

And Pierre, white of face, read on:

"So I got a idea that I had to write to you, Pierre. There ain't nothing I can make up to you, but knowing the truth may help some. Poor kid, you ain't got no father in the eyes of the law, and neither did you have no mother, and there ain't no name that belongs to you by rights.

"I was a man in them days, and your mother was a woman that brought your heart into your throat and set it singing. She and me, we were too busy being just plain happy to care much about what was right or wrong; so you just sort of happened along, Pierre. Me being so close to hell, I remember her eyes that was

8

bluer than heaven looking up to me, and her hair, that was copper with gold lights in it.

"I buried Irene on the side of the mountain under a big, rough rock, and I didn't carve nothing on the rock. Then I took you, Pierre, and I knew I wasn't no sort of a man to raise up the son of Irene; so I brought you to Father Victor on a winter night and left you in his arms. That was after I'd done my best to raise you and you was just about old enough to chatter a bit. There wasn't nothing else to do. My wife, she went pretty near crazy when I brought you home. And she'd of killed you, Pierre, if I hadn't took you away.

"You see, I was married before I met Irene. So there ain't no alibi for me. But me being so close to hell now, I look back to that time, and somehow I see no wrong in it still.

"And if I done wrong then, I've got my share of hell-fire for it. Here I lie, with my boys, Bill and Bert, sitting around in the corner of the room waiting for me to go out. They ain't men, Pierre. They're wolves in the skins of men. They're the right sons of their mother. When I go out they'll grab the coin I've saved up, and leave me to lie here and rot, maybe.

"Lad, it's a fearful thing to die without having no one around that cares, and to know that even after I've gone out I'm going to lie here and have my dead eyes looking up at the ceiling. So I'm writing to you, Pierre, part to tell you what you ought to know; part because I got a sort of crazy idea that maybe you could get down here to me before I go out.

"You don't owe me nothing but hard words, Pierre; but if you don't try to come to me, the ghost of your mother will follow you all your life, lad, and you'll be seeing her blue eyes and the red-gold of her hair in the dark of the night as I see it now. Me, I'm a hard man, but it breaks my heart, that ghost of Irene. So here I'll lie, waiting for you, Pierre, and lingering out the days with whisky, and fighting the wolf eyes of them there sons of mine. If I weaken—If they find they can look me square in the eye—they'll finish me quick and make off with the coin. Pierre, come quick.

MARTIN RYDER."

The hand of Pierre dropped slowly to his side, and the letter fluttered with a crisp rustling to the floor.

9

3

Then came a voice that startled the two priests, for it seemed that a fourth man had entered the room, so changed was it from the musical voice of Pierre.

"Father Victor, the roan is a strong horse. May I take him?"

"Pierre!" and the priest reached out his bony hands.

But the boy did not seem to notice or to understand.

"It is a long journey, and I will need a strong horse. It must be eight hundred miles to that town."

"Pierre, what claim has he upon you? What debt have you to repay?"

And Pierre le Rouge answered: "He loved my mother."

"You are going?"

The boy asked in astonishment: "Would you not have me go, Father?"

And Jean Paul Victor could not meet the sorrowful blue eyes.

He bowed his head and answered: "My child, I would have you go. But promise with your hand in mine that you will come back to me when your father is buried."

The lean fingers caught the extended hand of Pierre and froze about it.

"But first I have a second duty in the southland."

"A second?"

"You taught me to shoot and to use a knife. Once you said: 'An eye for an eye, and a tooth for a tooth.' Father Victor, my father was killed by another man."

"dear lad, swear to me here on this cross that you

will not raise your hands against the murderer. 'Vengeance is mine, saith the Lord.'"

"He must have an instrument for his wrath. He shall work through me in this."

"Pierre, you blaspheme."

"'An eye for an eye, and a tooth for a tooth.'"

"It was a demon in me that quoted that in your hearing, and not myself."

"The horse, Father Victor—may I have the roan?"

"Pierre, I command you—"

The light in the blue eyes was as cold and steady as that in the starved eyes of Jean Paul Victor.

"Hush!" he said calmly. "For the sake of the love that I bear for you, do not command me."

The stern priest dropped his head. He said at last: "I have nothing saving one great and terrible treasure which I see was predestined to you. It is the cross of Father Meilan. You have worn it before. You shall wear it hereafter as your own."

He took from his own neck a silver cross suspended by a slender silver chain, and the boy, with startled eyes, dropped to his knees and received the gift.

"It has brought good to all who possessed it, but for every good thing that it works for you it will work evil on some other. Great is its blessing and great is its burden. I, alas, know; but you also have heard of its history. Do you accept it, Pierre?"

"Dear Father, with all my heart."

The colorless hands touched the dark-red hair.

"God pardon the sins you shall commit."

Pierre crushed the hand of Jean Paul Victor against his lips and rushed from the room, while the tall priest, staring down at the fingers which had been kissed, pronounced: "I have forged a thunderbolt, Father Gabrielle. It is too great for my hand. Listen!"

And they heard clearly the sharp clang of a horse's hoofs on the hard-packed snow, loud at first, but fading rapidly away. The wind, increasing suddenly, shook the house furiously about them.

It was a north wind, and traveled south before the rider of the strong roan. Over a thousand miles of plain and hills it passed, and down into the cattle country of the mountain-desert which the Rockies hem on one side and the tall Sierras on the other.

It was a trail to try even the endurance of Pierre and the strong roan, but the boy clung to it doggedly. On a trail that led down from the edges of the northern mountain the roan crashed to the ground in a plunging fall, hitting heavily on his knees. He was dead before the boy had freed his feet from the stirrups.

Pierre threw the saddle over his shoulder and walked eight miles to the nearest ranch house, where he spent practically the last cent of his money on another horse, and drove on south once more.

There was little hope in him as day after day slipped past. Only the ghost of a chance remained that Martin Ryder could fight away death for another fortnight; yet Pierre had seen many a man from the mountain-desert stave off the end through weeks and weeks of the bitterest suffering. His father must be a man of the same hard durable metal, and upon that Pierre staked all his hopes.

And always he carried the picture of the dying man alone with his two wolf-eyed sons who waited for his eyes to weaken. Whenever he thought of that he touched his horse with the spurs and rode fiercely for a time. They were his flesh and blood, the man, and even the two wolf-eyed sons.

So he came at last to a gap in the hills and looked down on Morgantown in the hollow, twoscore unpainted houses sprawling along a single street. The snow was everywhere white and pure, and the town was like a stain on the landscape with wisps of smoke rising and trailing across the hilltops.

Down to the edge of the town he rode, left his cow-pony standing with hanging head outside a saloon, strode through the swinging doors, and asked of the bartender the way to the house of Martin Ryder.

The bartender stopped in his labor of rubbing down the surface of his bar and stared at the black-serge robe of the stranger, with curiosity rather than criticism, for women, madmen, and clergymen have the right-of-way in the mountain-desert.

He said: "Well, I'll be damned!—askin' your pardon. So old Mart Ryder has come down to this, eh? Partner, you're sure going to have a rough ride getting Mart to heaven. Better send a posse along with him, because some first-class angels are going to get considerable riled when they sight him coming. Ha, ha, ha! Sure I'll show you the way. Take the northwest road out of town and go five miles till you see a broken-backed shack lyin' over to the right. That's Mart Ryder's place."

Out to the broken-backed shack rode Pierre le Rouge, Pierre the Red, as everyone in the north country knew him. His second horse, staunch cow-pony that it was, stumbled on with sagging knees and hanging head, but Pierre rode upright, at ease, for his mind was untired.

Broken-backed indeed was the house before which he dismounted. The roof sagged from end to end, and the stove pipe chimney leaned at a drunken angle. Nature itself was withered beside that house; before the door stood a great cottonwood, gashed and scarred by lightning, with the limbs almost entirely stripped away from one side. Under this broken monster Pierre stepped and through the door. Two growls like the snarls of watch-dogs greeted him, and two tall, unshaven men barred his way.

13

Behind them, from the bed in the corner, a feeble voice called: "Who's there?"

"In the name of God," said the boy gravely, for he saw a hollow-eyed specter staring toward him from the bed in the corner, "let me pass! I am his son!"

It was not that which made them give back, but a shrill, faint cry of triumph from the sick man toward which they turned. Pierre slipped past them and stood above Martin Ryder. He was wasted beyond belief—only the monster hand showed what he had been.

"Son?" he queried with yearning and uncertainty.

"Pierre, your son."

And he slipped to his knees beside the bed. The heavy hand fell upon his hair and stroked it.

"There ain't no ways of doubting it. It's red silk, like the hair of Irene. Seein' you, boy, it ain't so hard to die. Look up! So! Pierre, my son! Are you scared of me, boy?"

"I'm not afraid."

"Not with them eyes you ain't. Now that you're here, pay the coyotes and let 'em go off to gnaw the bones."

He dragged out a small canvas bag from beneath the blankets and gestured toward the two lurkers in the corner.

"Take it, and be damned to you!"

A dirty, yellow hand seized the bag; there was a chortle of exultation, and the two scurried out of the room.

"Three weeks they've watched an' waited for me to go out, Pierre. Three weeks they've waited an' sneaked up to my bed an' sneaked away agin, seein' my eyes open."

Looking into their fierce fever brightness, Pierre understood why they had quailed. For the man, though wrecked beyond hope of living, was terrible still. The thick, gray stubble on his face could not hide altogether the hard lines of mouth and jaw, and on the wasted arm the hand was grotesquely huge. It was horror that widened the eyes of

14

Pierre as he looked at Martin Ryder; it was a grim happiness that made his lips almost smile.

"You've taken holy orders, lad?"

"No."

"But the black dress?"

"I'm only a novice. I've sworn no vows."

"And you don't hate me—you hold no grudge against me for the sake of your mother?"

Pierre took the heavy hand.

"Are you not my father? And my mother was happy with you. For her sake I love you."

"The good Father Victor. He sent you to me."

"I came of my own will. He would not have let me go."

"He—he would have kept my flesh and blood away from me?"

"Do not reproach him. He would have kept me from a sin."

"Sin? By God, boy, no matter what I've done, is it sin for my son to come to me? What sin?"

"The sin of murder!"

"Ha!"

"I have come to find McGurk."

4

Like some old father-bear watching his cub flash teeth against a stalking lynx, half proud and half fearful of such courage, so the dying cattleman looked at his son. Excitement set a high and dangerous color in his cheek.

"Pierre—brave boy! Look at me. I ain't no imitation man, even now, but I ain't a ghost of what I was. There wasn't no man I wouldn't of met fair and square with bare hands or with a gun. Maybe my hands was big, but they were fast on the draw. I've lived all my life with iron on the hip, and my six-gun has seven notches.

"But McGurk downed me fair and square. There wasn't no murder. I was out for his hide, and he knew it. I done the provokin', an' he jest done the finishin', that was all. It hurts me a lot to say it, but he's a better man than I was. A kid like you, why, he'd jest eat you, Pierre."

Pierre le Rouge smiled again. He felt a stern pride to be the son of this man.

"So that's settled," went on Martin Ryder, "an' a damned good thing it is. Son, you didn't come none too soon. I'm goin' out fast. There ain't enough light left in me so's I can see my own way. Here's all I ask: When I die touch my eyelids soft an' draw 'em shut—I've seen the look in a dead man's eyes. Close 'em, and I know I'll go to sleep an' have good dreams. And down in the middle of Morgantown is the buryin'-ground. I've ridden past it a thousand times an' watched a corner plot, where the grass grows quicker than it does anywheres else in the cemetery. Pierre, I'd die plumb easy if I knew I was goin' to sleep the rest of time in that place."

"It shall be done."

"But that corner plot, it would cost a pile, son. And I've no money. I gave what I had to them wolf-eyed boys, Bill an' Bert. Money was what they wanted, an' after I had Irene's son with me, money was the cheapest way of gettin' rid of 'em."

"I'll buy the plot."

"Have you got that much money, lad?"

"Yes," lied Pierre calmly.

The bright eyes grew dimmer and then fluttered close.

16

Pierre started to his feet, thinking that the end had come. But the voice began again, fainter, slowly.

"No light left inside of me, but dyin' this way is easy. There ain't no wind will blow on me after I'm dead, but I'll be blanketed safe from head to foot in cool, sweet-smellin' sod—the kind that has tangles of the roots of grass. There ain't no snow will reach to me where I lie. There ain't no sun will burn down to me. Dyin' like that is jest—goin' to sleep."

After that he said nothing for a time, and the late afternoon darkened slowly through the room.

As for Pierre, he did not move, and his mind went back. He did not see the bearded wreck who lay dying before him, but a picture of Irene, with the sun lighting her copper hair with places of burning gold, and a handsome young giant beside her. They rode together on some upland trail at sunset time, sharply framed against the bright sky.

There was a whisper below him: "Irene!"

And Pierre looked down to blankly staring eyes. He groaned, and dropped to his knees.

"I have come for you," said the whisper, "because the time has come, Irene. We have to ride out together. We have a long ways to go. Are you ready?"

"Yes," said Pierre.

"Thank God! It's a wonderful night. The stars are asking us out. Quick! Into your saddle. Now the spurs. So! We are alone and free, with the winds around us, and all that we have been forgotten behind us."

The eyes opened wide and stared up; without a stir in the great, gaunt body, he was dead. Pierre reverently drew the eyes shut. There were no tears in his eyes, but a feeling of hollowness about his heart. He straightened and looked about him and found that the room was quite dark.

So in the dimness Pierre fumbled, by force of habit, at

his throat, and found the cross which he wore by a silver chain about his throat. He held it in a great grip and closed his eyes and prayed. When he opened his eyes again it was almost deep night in the room, and Pierre had passed from youth to manhood. Through the gloom nothing stood out distinctly save the white face of the dead man, and from that Pierre looked quickly away.

One by one he numbered his obligations to Martin Ryder, and first and last he remembered the lie which had soothed his father. The money for that corner plot where the grass grew first in the spring of the year—where was he to find it? He fumbled in his pocket and found only a single coin.

He leaned back against the wall and strove to concentrate on the problem, but his thoughts wandered in spite of himself. Looking backward, he remembered all things much more clearly than when he had actually seen them. For instance, he recalled now that as he walked through the door the two figures which had started up to block his way had left behind them some playing-cards at the corner table. One of these cards had slipped from the edge of the board and flickered slowly to the floor.

With that memory the thoughts of Pierre le Rouge stopped. The picture of the falling card remained; all else went out in his mind like the snuffing of the candle. Then, as if he heard a voice directing him through the utter blackness of the room, he knew what he must do.

All his wealth was the single half-dollar piece in his pocket, and there was only one way in which that coin could be increased to the sum he would need to buy that corner plot, where the soul of old Martin Ryder could sleep long and deep.

From his brothers he would get no help. The least memory of those sallow, hungry faces convinced him of that.

There remained the gaming table. In the north country

he had watched men sit in a silent circle, smoking, drinking, with the flare of an oil-lamp against deep, seamed faces, and only the slip and whisper of card against card.

Cold conscience tapped the shoulder of Pierre, remembering the lessons of Father Victor, but a moment later his head went up and his eyes were shining through the dark. After all, the end justified the means.

A moment later he was laughing softly as a boy in the midst of a prank, and busily throwing off the robe of serge. Fumbling through the night he located the shirt and trousers he had seen hanging from a nail on the wall. Into these he slipped, and then went out under the open sky.

The rest had revived the strength of the tough little cow-pony, and he drove on at a gallop toward the twinkling lights of Morgantown. There was a new consciousness about Pierre as if he had changed his whole nature with his clothes. The sober sense of duty which had kept him in awe all his life like a lifted finger, was almost gone, and in its place was a joyous freedom.

For the first time he faintly realized what an existence other than that of a priest might be. Now for a brief moment he could forget the part of the subdued novice and become merely a man with nothing about him to distinguish him from other men, nothing to make heads turn at his approach and raise whispers as he passed.

It was a game, but he rejoiced in it as a girl does in her first masquerade. Tomorrow he must be grave and sober-footed and an example to other men; tonight he could frolic as he pleased.

So Pierre le Rouge tossed back his head and laughed up to the frosty stars. The loose sleeves and the skirts of the robe no longer entangled his limbs. He threw up his arms and shouted. A hillside caught the sound and echoed it back to him with a wonderful clearness, and up and down the long ravine beat the clatter of the flying hoofs. The whole world shouted and laughed and rode with him on Morgantown.

If the people in the houses that he passed had known they would have started up from their chairs and taken rifle and horse and chased after him on the trail. But how could they tell from the passing of those ringing hoofs that Pierre, the novice, was dead, and Red Pierre was born?

So they drowsed on about their comfortable fires, and Pierre drew rein with a jerk before the largest of Morgantown's saloons. He had to set his teeth before he could summon the resolution to throw open the door. It was done; he stepped inside, and stood blinking in the sudden rush of light against his face.

It was all bewildering at first; the radiance, the blue tangle of smoke, the storm of voices. For Muldoon's was packed from door to door. Coins rang in a steady chorus along the bar, and the crowd waited three and four deep.

Someone was singing a rollicking song of the range at one end of the bar, and a chorus of four bellowed a profane parody at the other end.

The ears of Pierre le Rouge tingled hotly, and partly to escape the uproar he worked his way to the quieter room at the back of the saloon.

It was almost as crowded as the bar, but here no one spoke except for an occasional growl. Sudden speaking, and a loud voice, indeed, was hardly safe. Someone cursed at his ill-luck as Pierre entered, and a dozen hands reached for six-guns. In such a place one had to be prepared.

Pierre remembered with quick dismay that he was not armed. All his life the straight black gown had been weapon enough to make all men give way before him. Now he carried no borrowed strength upon his shoulders.

Automatically he slipped his fingers under the breast of his shirt until their tips touched the cold metal of the cross. That gave him stronger courage. The joy of the adventure made his blood warm again as he drew out his one coin and looked for a place to start his venture.

So he approached the nearest table. On the surface of it were marked six squares with chalk, and each with its appropriate number. The man who ran the game stood behind the table and shook three dice. The numbers which turned up paid the gambler. The numbers which failed to show paid the owner of the game.

His luck had been too strong that night, and now only two men faced him, and both of them lost persistently. They were "bucking" the dice with savage stubbornness.

Pierre edged closer, shut his eyes, and deposited his coin. When he looked again he saw that he had wagered on the five.

5

The dice clattered across the table and were swept up by the hand of the man behind the table before Pierre could note them. Sick at heart, he began to turn away, as he saw that hand reach out and gather in the coins of the other two bettors. It went out a third time and laid another fifty-cent piece upon his. The heart of Pierre bounded up to his throat.

Again the dice rolled, and this time he saw distinctly two fives turn up. Two dollars in silver were dropped upon his, and still he let the money lie. Again, again, and again the dice rolled. And now there were pieces of gold among the silver that covered the square of the five.

The other two looked askance at him, and the owner of the game growled: "Gimme room for the coins, stranger, will you?"

Pierre picked up his winnings. In his left hand he held them, and the coins brimmed his cupped palm. With the free hand he placed his new wagers. But he lost now.

"I cannot win forever," thought Pierre, and redoubled his bets in an effort to regain the lost ground.

Still his little fortune dwindled, till the sweat came out on his forehead and the blood that had flushed his face ran back and left him pale with dread. And at last there remained only one gold piece. He hesitated, holding it poised for the wager, while the owner of the game rattled the dice loudly and looked up at the coin with hungry eyes.

Once more Pierre closed his eyes and laid his wager, while his empty left hand slipped again inside his shirt and touched the metal of the cross, and once more when he opened his eyes the hand of the gambler was going out to lay a second coin over his.

"It is the cross!" thought Pierre. "It is the cross which brings me luck."

The dice rattled out. He won. Again, and still he won. The gambler wiped his forehead and looked up anxiously. For these were wagers in gold, and the doubling stakes were running high. About Pierre a crowd had grown—a dozen cattlemen who watched the growing heap of gold with silent fascination. Then they began to make wagers of their own, and there were faint whispers of wrath and astonishment as the dice clicked out and each time the winnings of Pierre doubled.

Suddenly the dealer stopped and held up his left hand as a warning. With his right, very slowly, inch by inch lest anyone should suspect him of a gunplay, he drew out a heavy forty-five and laid it on the table with the belt of cartridges.

"Three years she's been on my hip through thick and thin, stranger. Three years she's shot close an' true. There ain't a butt in the world that hugs your hand tighter. There ain't a cylinder that spins easier. Shoot? Lad, even a kid like you could be a killer with that six-gun. What will you lay ag'in' it?"

And his red-stained eyes glanced covetously at the yellow heap of Pierre's money.

"How much?" said Pierre eagerly. "Is there enough on the table to buy the gun?"

"Buy?" said the other fiercely. "There ain't enough coin west of the Rockies to buy that gun. D'you think I'm yaller enough to sell my six? No, but I'll risk it in a fair bet. There ain't no disgrace in that; eh, pals?"

There was a chorus of low grunts of assent.·

"All right," said Pierre. "That pile against the gun."

"All of it?"

"All."

"Look here, kid, if you're tryin' to play a charity game with me—"

"Charity?"

The frank surprise of that look disarmed the other. He swept up the dice-box, and shook it furiously, while his lips stirred. It was as if he murmured an incantation for success. The dice rolled out, winking in the light, spun over, and the owner of the gun stood with both hands braced against the edge of the table, and stared hopelessly down.

A moment before his pockets had sagged with a precious weight, and there had been a significant drag of the belt over his right hip. Now both burdens were gone.

He looked up with a short laugh.

"I'm dry. Who'll stake me to a drink?"

Pierre scooped up a dozen pieces of the gold.

"Here."

The other drew back.

23

"You're very welcome to it. Here's more, if you'll have it."

"The coin I've lost to you? Take back a gamblin' debt?"

"Easy there," said one of the men. "Don't you see the kid's green? Here's a five-spot."

The loser accepted the coin as carelessly as if he were conferring a favor by taking it, cast another scowl in the direction of Pierre, and went out toward the bar. Pierre, very hot in the face, pocketed his winnings and belted on the gun. It hung low on his thigh, just in easy gripping distance of his hand, and he fingered the butt with a smile.

"The kid's feelin' most a man," remarked a sarcastic voice. "Say, kid, why don't you try your luck with Mac Hurley? He's almost through with poor old Cochrane."

Following the direction of the pointing finger, Pierre saw one of those mute tragedies of the gambling hall. Cochrane, an old cattleman whose carefully trimmed, pointed white beard and slender, tapering fingers set him apart from the others in the room, was rather far gone with liquor. He was still stiffly erect in his chair, and would be till the very moment consciousness left him, but his eyes were misty, and when he spoke his lips moved slowly, as though numbed by cold.

Beside him stood a tall, black bottle with a little whisky glass to flank it. He made his bets with apparent carelessness, but with a real and deepening gloom. Once or twice he glanced up sharply as though reckoning his losses, though it seemed to Pierre le Rouge almost like an appeal.

And what appeal could affect Mac Hurley? There was no color in the man, either body or soul. No emotion could show in those pale, small eyes or change the color of the flabby cheeks. If his hands had been cut off, he might have seemed some sodden victim of a drug habit, but the hands saved him.

They seemed to belong to another body—beautiful,

swift, and strong, and grafted by some foul mischance onto this rotten hulk. Very white they were, and long, with a nervous uneasiness in every motion, continually hovering around the cards with little touches which were almost caresses.

"It ain't a game," said the man who had first pointed out the group to Pierre, "it's just a slaughter. Cochrane's too far gone to see straight. Look at that deal now! A kid could see that he's crooking the cards!"

It was blackjack, and Hurley, as usual, was dealing. He dealt with one hand, flipping the cards out with a snap of the wrist, the fingers working rapidly over the pack. Now and then he glanced over to the crowd, as if to enjoy their admiration of his skill. He was showing it now, not so much by the deftness of his cheating as by the openness with which he exposed his tricks.

As the stranger remarked to Pierre, a child could have discovered that the cards were being dealt at will from the top and the bottom of the pack, but the gambler was enjoying himself by keeping his game just open enough to be apparent to every other man in the room—just covert enough to deceive the drink-misted brain of Cochrane. And the pale, swinish eyes twinkled as they stared across the dull sorrow of the old man. There was an ominous sound from Pierre: "Do you let a thing like that happen in this country?" he asked fiercely.

The other turned to him with a sneer.

"*Let* it happen? Who'll stop him? Say, partner, you ain't meanin' to say that you don't know who Hurley is?"

"I don't need telling. I can see."

"What you can't see means a lot more than what you can. I've been in the same room when Hurley worked his gun once. It wasn't any killin', but it was the prettiest bit of cheatin' I ever seen. But even if Hurley wasn't enough, what about Carl Diaz?"

He glared his triumph at Pierre, but the latter was too

25

puzzled to quail, and too stirred by the pale, gloomy face of Cochrane to turn toward the other.

"What of Diaz?"

"Look here, boy. You're a kid, all right, but you ain't that young. D'you mean to say that you ain't heard of Carlos Diaz?"

It came back to Pierre then, for even into the snow-bound seclusion of the north country the shadow of the name of Diaz had gone. He could not remember just what they were, but he seemed to recollect grim tales through which that name figured.

The other went on: "But if you ain't ever seen him before, look him over now. They's some says he's faster on the draw than Bob McGurk, but, of course, that's stretchin' him out a size too much. What's the matter, kid; you've met McGurk?"

"No, but I'm going to."

"Might even be carried to him, eh—feet first?"

Pierre turned and laid a hand on the shoulder of the other.

"Don't talk like that," he said gently. "I don't like it."

The other reached up to snatch the hand from his shoulder, but he stayed his arm.

He said after an uncomfortable moment of that silent staring: "Well, partner, there ain't a hell of a lot to get sore over, is there? You don't figure you're a mate for McGurk, do you?"

He seemed oddly relieved when the eyes of Pierre moved away from him and returned to the figure of Carlos Diaz. The Mexican was a perfect model for a painting of a melodramatic villain. He had waxed and twirled the end of his black mustache so that it thrust out a little spur on either side of his long face. His habitual expression was a scowl; his habitual position was with a cigarette in the fingers of his left hand, and his right hand resting on his hip.

He sat in a chair directly behind that of Hurley, and Pierre's new-found acquaintance explained: "He's the bodyguard for Hurley. Maybe there's some who could down Hurley in a straight gunfight; maybe there's one or two like McGurk that could down Diaz—damn his yellow hide—but there ain't no one can buck the two of 'em. It ain't in reason. So they play the game together. Hurley works the cards and Diaz covers up the retreat. Can't beat that, can you?"

Pierre le Rouge slipped his left hand once more inside his shirt until the fingers touched the cross.

"Nevertheless, that game has to stop."

"Who'll—say, kid, are you stringin' me, or are you drunk? Look me in the eye!"

6

Pierre turned and looked calmly upon the other.

And the man whispered in a sort of awe: "Well, I'll be damned!"

"Stand aside!"

The other fell back a pace, and Pierre went straight to the table and said to Cochrane: "Sir, I have come to take you home."

The old man looked up and rubbed his eyes as though waking from a sleep.

"Stand back from the table!" warned Hurley.

"By the Lord, have they been missing me?" queried old Cochrane.

"You are waited for," answered Pierre le Rouge, "and I've been sent to take you home."

"If that's the case—"

"It ain't the case. The kid's lying."

"Lying?" repeated Cochrane, as if he had never heard the word before, and he peered with clearing eyes toward Pierre. "No, I think this boy has never lied."

Silence had spread through the place like a vapor. Even the slight sounds in the gaming-room were done now, and one pair after another of eyes swung toward the table of Cochrane and Hurley. The wave of the silence reached to the barroom. No one could have carried the tidings so soon, but the air was surcharged with the consciousness of an impending crisis.

Half a dozen men started to make their way on tiptoe toward the back room. One stood with his whisky glass suspended in midair, and tilted back his head to listen. In the gaming-room Hurley pushed back his chair and leaned to the left, giving him a free sweep for his right hand. The Mexican smiled with a slow and deep content.

"Thank you," answered Pierre, "but I am waiting still, sir."

The left hand of Hurley played impatiently on the table.

He said: "Of course, if you have enough—"

"I—enough?" flared the old aristocrat.

Pierre le Rouge turned fairly upon Hurley.

"In the name of God," he said calmly, "make an end of your game. You're playing for money, but I think this man is playing for his eternal soul."

The solemn, bookish phraseology came smoothly from his tongue. He knew no other. It drew a murmur of amusement from the room and a snarl from Hurley.

"Put on skirts, kid, and join the Salvation Army, but don't get yourself messed all up in here. This is my party, and I'm damned particular who I invite! Now, run along!"

The head of Pierre tilted back, and he burst into laughter which troubled even Hurley.

The gambler blurted: "What's happening to you, kid?"

"I've been making a lot of good resolutions, Mr. Hurley, about keeping out of trouble; but here I am in it up to the neck."

"No trouble as long as you keep your hand out of another man's game, kid."

"That's it. I can't see you rob Mr. Cochrane like this. You aren't gambling—you're digging gold. The game stops now."

It was a moment before the crowd realized what was about to happen; they saw it reflected first in the face of Hurley, which suddenly went taut and pale, and then, even as they looked with a smile of curiosity and derision toward Pierre le Rouge, they saw and understood.

For the moment Pierre said, "The game stops now," the calm which had been with him was gone. It was like the scent of blood to the starved wolf. The last word was scarcely off his tongue when he was crouched with a devil of green fury in his eyes—the light struck his hair into a wave of flame—his face altered by a dozen ugly years.

"D'you mean?" whispered Hurley, as if he feared to break the silence with his full voice.

"Get out of the room."

And the impulse of Hurley, plainly enough, was to obey the order, and go anywhere to escape from that relentless stare. His glance wavered and flashed around the circle and then back to Red Pierre, for the expectancy of the crowd forced him back.

When the leader of the pack springs and fails to kill, the rest of the pack tear him to pieces. Remembering this, Mac Hurley forced his glance back to Pierre. Moreover, there was a soft voice from behind, and he remembered Diaz.

All this had taken place in the length of time that it takes a heavy body to totter on the brink of a precipice or a cat to regain its feet after a fall. After the voice of Diaz there was a sway through the room, a pulse of silence, and then three hands shot for their hips—Pierre, Diaz, and Hurley.

No stop-watch could have caught the differing lengths of time which each required for the draw. The muzzle of Hurley's revolver was not clear of the holster—the gun of Diaz was nearly at the level when Pierre's weapon exploded at his hip. The bullet cut through the wrist of Hurley. Never again would that slender, supple hand fly over the cards, doing things other than they seemed. He made no effort to escape from the next bullet, but stood looking down at his broken wrist; horror for the moment gave him a dignity oddly out of place with his usual appearance. He alone in all the room was moveless.

The crowd, undecided for an instant, broke for the doors at the first shot; Pierre le Rouge pitched to the floor as Diaz leaped forward, the revolver in either hand spitting lead and fire.

It was no bullet that downed Pierre but his own cunning. He broke his fall with an outstretched left hand, while the bullets of Diaz pumped into the void space which his body had filled a moment before.

Lying there at ease, he leveled the revolver, grinning with the mirthless lust of battle, and fired over the top of the table. The guns dropped from the hands of huge Diaz. He caught at his throat and staggered back the full length of the room, crashing against the wall. When he pitched forward on his face he was dead before he struck the floor.

Pierre, now Red Pierre, indeed, rose and ran to the fallen man, and, looking at the bulk of the giant, he wondered with a cold heart. He knew before he slipped his hand over the breast of Diaz that this was death. Then he rose again and watched the still fingers which seemed to be gripping at the boards.

These he saw, and nothing else, and all he heard was the rattling of the wind of winter, wrenching at some loose shingle on the roof, and he knew that he was alone in the world, for he had put out a life.

He found a strange weight pulling down his right hand, and started when he saw the revolver. He replaced it in the holster automatically, and in so doing touched the barrel and found it warm.

Then fear came to Pierre, the first real fear of his life. He jerked his head high and looked about him. The room was utterly empty. He tiptoed to the door and found even the long bar deserted, littered with tall bottles and over-turned glasses. The cold in his heart increased. A moment before he had been hand in hand with all the mirth in that place.

Now the men whose laughter he had repeated with smiles, the men against whose sleeves his elbow had touched, were further away from him than they had been when all the snow-covered miles from Morgantown to the school of Father Victor had laid between them. They were men who might lose themselves in any crowd, but he was set apart with a brand, even as Hurley and Diaz had been set apart that eventful evening.

He had killed a man. That fact blotted out the world. He drew his gun again and stole down the length of the bar. Once he stopped and poised the weapon before he realized that the white, fierce face that squinted at him was his own reflection in a mirror.

Outside the door the free wind caught at his face, and he blessed it in his heart, as if it had been the touch of the hand of a friend. Beyond the long, dark, silent street the moor rose and passed up through the safe, dark spaces of the sky.

He must move quickly now. The pursuit was not yet organized, but it would begin in a space of minutes. From the group of half a dozen horses which stood before the saloon he selected the best—a tall, raw-boned nag with an ugly head. Into the saddle he swung, wondering faintly that the theft of a horse mattered so little to him. His was the greatest sin. All other things mattered nothing.

Down the long street he galloped. The sharp echoes flew out at him from every unlighted house, but not a human being was in sight. So he swung out onto the long road which wound up through the hills, and beside him rode a grim brotherhood, the invisible fellowship of Cain.

The moon rose higher, brighter, and a grotesque black shadow galloped over the snow beside him. He turned his head sharply to the other side and watched the sweep of white hills which reached back in range after range until they blended with the shadows of night.

The road faded to a bridle path, and this in turn he lost among the windings of the valley. He was lost from even the traces of men, and yet the fear of men pursued him. Fear, and yet with it there was a thrill of happiness, for every swinging stride of the tall, wild roan carried him deeper into freedom, the unutterable fierce freedom of the hunted.

7

All life was tame compared with this sudden awakening of Pierre. He had killed a man. For fear of it he raced the tall roan furiously through the night.

He had killed a man. For the joy of it he shouted a song

that went ringing across the blank, white hills. What place was there in Red Pierre for solemn qualms of conscience? Had he not met the first and last test triumphantly? The oldest instinct in creation was satisfied in him. Now he stood ready to say to all the world: Behold, a man!

Let it be remembered that his early years had been passed in a dull, dun silence, and time had slipped by him with softly padding, uneventful hours. Now, with the rope of restraint snapped, he rode at the world with hands, palm upward, asking for life, and that life which lies under the hills of the mountain-desert heard his question and sent a cold, sharp echo back to answer his lusty singing.

The first answer, as he plunged on, not knowing where, and not caring, was when the roan reeled suddenly and flung forward to the ground. Even that violent stop did not unseat Red Pierre. He jerked up on the reins with a curse and drove in the spurs. Valiantly the horse reared his shoulders up, but when he strove to rise the right foreleg dangled helplessly. He had stepped in some hole and the bone was broken cleanly across.

The rider slipped from the saddle and stood facing the roan, which pricked its ears forward and struggled once more to regain its feet. The effort was hopeless, and Pierre took the broken leg and felt the rough edges of the splintered bone through the skin. The animal, as if it sensed that the man was trying to do it some good, nosed his shoulder and whinnied softly.

Pierre stepped back and drew his revolver. The bullet would do quickly what the cold would accomplish after lingering hours of torture, yet, facing those pricking ears and the trust of the eyes, he was blinded by a mist and could not aim. He had to place the muzzle of the gun against the roan's temple and pull the trigger. When he turned his back he was the only living thing within the white arms of the hills.

Yet, when the next hill was behind him, he had already forgotten the second life which he put out that night, for regret is the one sorrow which never dodges the footsteps of the hunted. Like all his brotherhood of Cain, Pierre le Rouge pressed forward across the mountain-desert with his face turned toward the brave tomorrow. In the evening of his life, if he should live to that time, he would walk and talk with God.

Now he had no mind save for the bright day coming.

He had been riding with the wind and had scarcely noticed its violence in his headlong course. Now he felt it whipping sharply at his back and increasing with each step. Overhead the sky was clear. It seemed to give vision for the wind and cold to seek him out, and the moon made his following shadow long and black across the snow.

The wind quickened rapidly to a gale that cut off the surface of the snow and whipped volleys of the small particles level with the surface. It cut the neck of Red Pierre, and the gusts struck his shoulders with staggering force like separate blows, twisting him a little from side to side.

Coming from the direction of Morgantown, it seemed as if the vengeance for Diaz was following the slayer. Once he turned and laughed in the teeth of the wind, and shook his fist back at Morgantown and all the avenging powers of the law.

Yet he was glad to turn away from the face of the storm and stride on down-wind. Even traveling with the gale grew more and more impossible. The snowdrifts which the wind picked up and hurried across the hills pressed against Pierre's back like a great, invisible hand, bowing him as if beneath a burden. In the hollows the labor was not so great, but when he approached a summit the gale screamed in his ear and struck him savagely.

For all his optimism, for all his young, undrained strength, a doubt began to grow in the mind of Pierre le

Rouge. At length, remembering how that weight of gold came in his pockets, he slipped his left hand into the bosom of his shirt and touched the icy metal of the cross. Almost at once he heard, or thought he heard, a faint, sweet sound of singing.

The heart of Red Pierre stopped. For he knew the visions which came to men perishing with cold; but he grew calmer again in a moment. This touch of cold was nothing compared with whole months of hard exposure which he had endured in the northland. It had not the edge. If it were not for the wind it was scarcely a threat to life. Moreover, the singing sounded no more. It had been hardly more than a phrase of music, and it must have been a deceptive murmur of the wind.

After all, a gale brought wilder deceptions than that. Some men had actually heard voices declaiming words in such a wind. He himself had heard them tell their stories. So he leaned forward again and gave his stanch heart to the task. Yet once more he stopped, for this time the singing came clearly, sweetly to him.

There was no doubt of it now. Of course it was wildly impossible, absurd; but beyond all question he heard the voice of a girl come whistling down the wind. He could almost catch the words. For a little moment he lingered still. Then he turned and fought his way into the strong arms of the storm.

Every now and then he paused and crouched to the snow. Usually there was only the shriek of the wind in his ears, but a few times the singing came to him and urged him on. If he had allowed the idea of failure to enter his mind, he must have given up the struggle, but failure was a stranger to his thoughts.

He lowered his head against the storm. Sometimes it caught under him and nearly lifted him from his feet. But he clung against the slope of the hill, sometimes gripping hard with his hands. So he worked his way to the right, the sound of the singing coming more and more frequently and louder and louder. When he was almost upon the source of the music it ceased abruptly.

He waited a moment, but no sound came. He struggled forward a few more yards and pitched down exhausted, panting. Still he heard the singing no longer. With a falling heart he rose and resigned himself to wander on his original course with the wind, but as he started he placed his hand once more against the cross, and it was then that he saw her.

For he had simply gone past her, and the yelling of the storm had cut off the sound of her voice. Now he saw her lying, a spot of bright color on the snow. He read the story at a glance. As she passed this steep-sided hill the loosely piled snow had slid down and carried with it the dead trunk of a fallen tree.

Pierre came from behind and stood over her unnoticed. He saw that the oncoming tree, by a strange chance, had knocked down the girl and pinned her legs to the ground. His strength and the strength of a dozen men would not be sufficient to release her. This he saw at the first glance, and saw the bright gold of her hair against the snow. Then he dropped on his knees beside her.

8

The girl tossed up her arms in a silent greeting, and Pierre caught the small cold hands and saw that she was only a child of twelve or fourteen trapped by the wild storm sweeping over them.

He crouched lower still, and when he did so the strength of the wind against his face decreased wonderfully, for the sharp angle of the hill's declivity protected them. Seeing him kneel there, she cried out with a little wail: "Help me—the tree—help me!" And, bursting into a passion of sobbing, she tugged her hands from his and covered her face.

Pierre placed his shoulder under the trunk and lifted till the muscles of his back snapped and cracked. He could not budge the weight; he could not even send a tremor through the mass of wood. He dropped back beside her with a groan. He felt her eyes upon him; she had ceased her sobs, and looked steadily into his face.

It would have been easy for him to meet that look on the morning of this day, but after that night's work in Morgantown he had to brace his nerve to withstand it.

She said: "You can't budge the tree?"

"Yes—in a minute; I will try again."

"You'll only hurt yourself for nothing. I saw how you strained at it."

The greatest miracle he had ever seen was her calm. Her eyes were wide and sorrowful indeed, but she was almost smiling up to him.

After a while he was able to say, in a faint voice: "Are you very cold?"

She answered: "I'm not afraid. But if you stay longer with me, you may freeze. The snow and even the tree help to keep me almost warm; but you will freeze. Go for help; hurry, and if you can, send it back to me."

He thought of the long miles back to Morgantown; no human being could walk that distance against this wind; not even a strong horse could make its way through the storm. If he went on with the wind, how long would it be before he reached a house? Before him, over range after range of hills, he saw no single sign of a building. If he reached some such place it would be the same story as the trip to Morgantown; men simply could not beat a way against that wind.

Then a cold hand touched him, and he looked up to find her eyes grave and wide once more, and her lips half smiling, as if she strove to deceive him.

"There's no chance of bringing help?"

He merely stared hungrily at her, and the loveliest thing he had ever seen was the play of golden hair beside her cheek. Her smile went out. She withdrew her hand, but she repeated: "I'm not afraid. I'll simply grow numb and then fall asleep. But you go on and save yourself."

Seeing him shake his head, she caught his hands again.

"I'll be unhappy. You'll make me so unhappy if you stay. Please go."

He raised the small hand and pressed it to his lips.

She said: "You are crying!"

"No, no!"

"There! I see the tears shining on my hand. What is your name?"

"Pierre."

"Pierre? I like that name. Pierre, to make me happy, will you go? Your face is all white and touched with a shadow of blue. It is the cold. Oh, won't you go?" Then she pleaded, finding him obdurate: "If you won't go for me, then go for your father."

He raised his head with a sudden laughter, and, raising it, the wind beat into his face fiercely and the particles of snow whipped his skin.

"Dear Pierre, then for your mother?"

He bowed his head.

"Not for all the people who love you and wait for you now by some warm fire—some cozy fire, all yellow and bright?"

He took her hands and with them covered his eyes.

"Listen: I have no father; I have no mother."

"Pierre! Oh, Pierre, I'm sorry!"

"And for the rest of 'em, I've killed a man. The whole world hates me; the whole world's hunting me."

The small hands tugged away. He dared not raise his bowed head for fear of her eyes. And then the hands came back to him and touched his face.

She was saying tremulously: "Then he deserved to be killed. There must be men like that—almost. And I—like you still, Pierre."

"Really?"

"I almost think I like you more—because you could kill a man—and then stay here for me."

"If you were a grown-up girl, do you know what I'd say?"

"Please tell me."

"That I could love you."

"Pierre—"

"Yes."

"My name is Mary Brown."

He repeated several times: "Mary."

"And if I were a grown-up girl, do you know what I would answer?"

"I don't dare guess it."

"That I could love you, Pierre, if you were a grown-up man."

"But I am."

"Not a really one."

And they both broke into laughter—laughter that died out before a sound of rushing and of thunder, as a mass slid swiftly past them, snow and mud and sand and rubble. The wind fell away from them, and when Pierre looked up he saw that a great mass of tumbled rock and soil loomed above them.

The landslide had not touched them, by some miracle,

39

but in a moment more it might shake loose again, and all that mass of ton upon ton of stone and loam would overwhelm them. The whole mass quaked and trembled, and the very hillside shuddered beneath them.

She looked up and saw the coming ruin; but her cry was for him, not herself.

"Run, Pierre—you can save yourself."

With that terror threatening him from above, he rose and started to run down the hill. A moan of woe followed him, and he stopped and turned back, and fought his way through the wind until he was beside her once more.

She was weeping.

"Pierre—I couldn't help calling out for you; but now I'm strong again, and I won't have you stay. The whole mountain is shaking and falling toward us. Go now, Pierre, and I'll never make a sound to bring you back."

He said: "Hush! I've something here which will keep us both safe. Look!"

He tore from the chain the little metal cross, and held it high overhead, glimmering in the pallid light. She forgot her fear in wonder.

"I gambled with only one coin to lose, and I came out tonight with hundreds and hundreds of dollars because I had the cross. It is a charm against all danger and against all bad fortune. It has never failed me."

Over them the piled mass slid closer. The forehead of Pierre gleamed with sweat, but a strong purpose made him talk on. At least he could take all the foreboding of death from the child, and when the end came it would be swift and wipe them both out at one stroke. She clung to him, eager to believe.

"I've closed my eyes so that I can believe."

"It has never failed me. It saved me when I fought two men. One of them I crippled and the other died. You see, the power of the cross is as great as that. Do you doubt it now, Mary?"

40

"Do you believe in it so much—really—Pierre?"

Each time there was a little lowering of her voice, a little pause and caress in the tone as she uttered his name, and nothing in all his life had stirred Red Pierre so deeply with happiness and sorrow.

"Do you believe, Pierre?" she repeated.

He looked up and saw the shuddering mass of the landslide creeping upon them inch by inch. In another moment it would loose itself with a rush and cover them.

"I believe," he said.

"If you should live, and I should die—"

"I would throw the cross away."

"No, you would keep it; and every time you touched it you would think of me, Pierre, would you not?"

"When you reach out to me like that, you take my heart between your hands."

"And I feel grown up and sad and happy both together. After we've been together on such a night, how can we ever be apart again?"

The mass of the landslide toppled right above them. She did not seem to see.

"I'm so happy, Pierre. I was never so happy."

And he said, with his eyes on the approaching ruin: "It was your singing that brought me to you. Will you sing again?"

"I sang because I knew that when I sang the sound would carry farther through the wind than if I called for help. What shall I sing for you now, Pierre?"

"What you sang when I came to you."

And the light, sweet voice rose easily through the sweep of the wind. She smiled as she sang, and the smile and music were all for Pierre, he knew. Through the last stanza of the song the rumble of the approaching death grew louder, and as she ended he threw himself beside her and gathered her into protecting arms.

She cried: "Pierre! What is it?"

41

"I must keep you warm; the snow will eat away your strength."

"No; it's more than that. Tell me, Pierre! You don't trust the power of the cross?"

"Are you afraid?"

"Oh, no; I'm not afraid, Pierre."

"If one life would be enough, I'd give mine a thousand times. Mary, we are to die."

An arm slipped around his neck—a cold hand pressed against his cheek.

"Pierre."

"Yes."

The thunder broke above them with a mighty roaring.

"*You* have no fear."

"Mary, if I had died alone I would have dropped down to hell under my sins; but, with your arm around me, you'll take me with you. Hold me close."

"With all my heart, Pierre. See—I'm not afraid. It is like going to sleep. What wonderful dreams we'll have!"

And then the black mass of the landslide swept upon them.

9

Down all the length of the mountain-desert and across its width of rocks and mountains and valleys and stern plateaus there is a saying: "You can tell a man by the horse he rides." For most other important things are apt to go by opposites, which is the usual way in which a man selects his wife. With dogs, for instance—a quiet man is apt to want an active dog, and a tractable fellow may keep the most vicious of wolf-dogs.

But when it comes to a horse, a man's heart speaks for itself, and if he has sufficient knowledge he will choose a sympathetic mount. A woman loves a neat-stepping saddle-horse; a philosopher likes a nodding, stumble-footed nag which will jog all day long and care not a whit whether it goes up dale or down.

To know the six wild riders who galloped over the white reaches of the mountain-desert this night, certainly their horses should be studied first and the men secondly, for the one explained the other.

They came in a racing triangle. Even the storm at its height could not daunt such furious riders. At the point of the triangle thundered a mighty black stallion, his muzzle and his broad chest flecked with white foam, for he stretched his head out and champed at the bit with ears laid flat back, as though even that furious pace gave him no opportunity to use fully his strength.

He was an ugly headed monster with a savagely hooked Roman nose and small, keen eyes, always red at the corners. A medieval baron in full panoply of plate armor would have chosen such a charger among ten thousand steeds, yet the black stallion needed all his strength to uphold the unarmored giant who bestrode him, a savage figure.

When the broad brim of his hat flapped up against the wind the moonshine caught at shaggy brows, a cruelly arched nose, thin, straight lips, and a forward-thrusting jaw. It seemed as if nature had hewn him roughly and designed him for a primitive age where he could fight his way with hands and teeth.

This was Jim Boone. To his right and a little behind him galloped a riderless horse, a beautiful young animal continually tossing its head and looking as if for guidance at the big stallion.

To the left strode a handsome bay with pricking ears. A mound interfered with his course, and he cleared it in magnificent style that would have brought a cheer from the lips of any English lover of the chase.

Straight in the saddle sat Dick Wilbur, and he raised his face a little to the wind, smiling faintly as if he rejoiced in its fine strength, as handsome as the horse he rode, as cleanly cut, as finely bred. The moon shone a little brighter on him than on any other of the six riders.

Bud Mansie behind, for instance, kept his head slightly to one side and cursed beneath his breath at the storm and set his teeth at the wind. His horse, delicately formed, with long, slender legs, could not have endured that charge against the storm save that it constantly edged behind the leaders and let them break the wind. It carried less weight than any other mount of the six, and its strength was cunningly nursed by the rider so that it kept its place, and at the finish it would be as strong as any and swifter, perhaps, for a sudden, short effort, just as Bud Mansie might be numbed through all his nervous, slender body, but never too numb for swift and deadly action.

On the opposite wing of the flying wedge galloped a dust-colored gray, ragged of mane and tail, and vindictive of eye, like its down-headed rider, who shifted his glance rapidly from side to side and watched the ground closely before his horse as if he were perpetually prepared for danger.

He distrusted the very ground over which his mount strode. For all this he seemed the least formidable of all the riders. To see him pass none could have suspected that this was Black Morgan Gandil.

Last of the crew came two men almost as large as Jim Boone himself, on strong steady-striding horses. They came last in this crew, but among a thousand other long-riders they would have ridden first, either red-faced, good-humored, loud-voiced Garry Patterson, or Phil Branch, stout-handed, blunt of jaw, who handled men as he had once hammered red iron at the forge.

Each of them should have ridden alone in order to be properly appreciated. To see them together was like watching a flock of eagles every one of which should have been a solitary lord of the air. But after scanning that lordly train which followed, the more terrible seemed the rider of the great black horse.

Yet the king was sad, and the reason for his sadness was the riderless horse which galloped so freely beside him. His son had ridden that horse when they set out, and all the way down to the railroad Handsome Hal Boone had kept his mount prancing and curveting and had ridden around and around tall Dick Wilbur, playing pranks, and had teased his father's black until the big stallion lashed out wildly with furious heels.

It was the memory of this that kept the grave shadow of a smile on the father's lips for all the sternness of his eyes. He never turned his head, for, looking straight forward, he could conjure up the laughing vision; but when he glanced to the empty saddle he heard once more the last unlucky shot fired from the train as they raced off with their booty, and saw Hal reel in his saddle and pitch forward; and how he had tried to check his horse and turn back; and how Dick Wilbur, and Patterson, and big Phil Branch had forced him to go on and leave that form lying motionless on the snow.

At that he groaned, and spurred the black, and so the cavalcade rushed faster and faster through the night.

They came over a sharp ridge and veered to the side just in time, for all the further slope was a mass of treacherous sand and rubble and raw rocks and mud, where a landslide had stripped the hill to the stone.

As they veered about the ruin and thundered on down

to the foot of the hill, Jim Boone threw up his hand for a signal and brought his stallion to a halt on back-braced, sliding legs.

For a metallic glitter had caught his eye, and then he saw, half covered by the pebbles and dirt, the figure of a man. He must have been struck by the landslide and not over-whelmed by it, but rather carried before it like a stick in a rush of water. At the outermost edge of the wave he lay with the rocks and dirt washed over him. Boone swung from the saddle and lifted Pierre le Rouge.

The gleam of metal was the cross which his fingers still gripped. Boone examined it with a somewhat superstitious caution, took it from the nerveless fingers, and slipped it into a pocket of Pierre's shirt. A small cut on the boy's forehead showed where the stone struck which knocked him senseless, but the cut still bled—a small trickle—Pierre lived. He even stirred and groaned and opened his eyes, large and deeply blue.

It was only an instant before they closed, but Boone had seen. He turned with the figure lifted easily in his arms as if Pierre had been a child fallen asleep by the hearth and now about to be carried off to bed.

And the outlaw said: "I've lost my boy tonight. This here one was given me by the will of—God."

Black Morgan Gandil reined his horse close by, leaned to peer down, and the shadow of his hat fell across the face of Pierre.

"There's no good comes of savin' shipwrecked men. Leave him where you found him, Jim. That's my advice. Sidestep a redheaded man. That's what I say."

The quick-stepping horse of Bud Mansie came near, and the rider wiped his stiff lips, and spoke from the side of his mouth, a prison habit of the line that moves in the lockstep: "Take it from me, Jim, there ain't any place in our crew for a man you've picked up without knowing him beforehand. Let him lay, I say."

But big Dick Wilbur was already leading up the horse of Hal Boone, and into the saddle Jim Boone swung the inert body of Pierre. The argument was settled, for every man of them knew that nothing could turn Boone back from a thing once begun. Yet there were muttered comments that drew Black Morgan Gandil and Bud Mansie together.

And Gandil, from the South Seas, growled with averted eyes: "This is the most fool stunt the chief has ever pulled."

"Right, pal," answered Mansie. "You take a snake in out of the cold, and it bites you when it comes to in the warmth; but the chief has started, and there ain't nothing that'll make him stop, except maybe God or McGurk."

And Black Gandil answered with his evil, sudden grin: "Maybe McGurk, but not God."

They started on again with Garry Patterson and Dick Wilbur riding close on either side of Pierre, supporting his limp body. It delayed the whole gang, for they could not go on faster than a jog-trot. The wind, however, was falling off in violence. Its shrill whistling ceased, at length, and they went on, accompanied only by the harsh crunching of the snow underfoot.

10

Consciousness returned to Pierre slowly. Many a time his eyes opened, and he saw nothing, but when he did see and hear it was by vague glimpses.

He heard the crunch of the snow underfoot; he heard the panting and snorting of the horses; he felt the swing and jolt of the saddle beneath him; he saw the grim faces of the long-riders, and he said: "The law has taken me."

Thereafter he let his will lapse, and surrendered to the sleepy numbness which assailed his brain in waves. He was riding without support by this time, but it was an automatic effort. There was no more real life in him than in a dummy figure. It was not the effect of the blow. It was rather the long exposure and the overexertion of mind and body during the evening and night. He had simply collapsed beneath the strain.

But an old army man has said: "Give me a soldier of eighteen or twenty. In a single day he may not march quite so far as a more mature man or carry quite so much weight. He will go to sleep each night dead to the world. But in the morning he awakens a new man. He is like a slate from which all the writing has been erased. He is ready for a new day and a new world. Thirty days of campaigning leaves him as strong and fresh as ever.

"Thirty days of campaigning leaves the old soldier a wreck. Why? Because as a man grows older he loses the ability to sleep soundly. He carries the nervous strain of one day over to the next. Life is a serious problem to a man over thirty. To a man under thirty it is simply a game. For my part, give me men who can play at war."

So it was with Pierre le Rouge. He woke with a faint heaviness of head, and stretched himself. There were many sore places, but nothing more. He looked up, and the slant winter sun cut across his face and made a patch of bright yellow on the wall beside him.

Next he heard a faint humming, and, turning his head, saw a boy of fourteen or perhaps a little more, busily cleaning a rifle in a way that betokened the most expert knowledge of the weapon. Pierre himself knew rifles as a preacher knows his Bible, and as he lay half awake and half asleep he smiled with enjoyment to see the deft fingers move here and there, wiping away the oil. A green hand will spend half a day cleaning a gun, and then do the work imperfectly; an expert does the job efficiently in ten minutes. This was an expert.

Undoubtedly this was a true son of the mountain-desert. He wore his old slouch hat even in the house, and his skin was that olive brown which comes from many years of exposure to the wind and sun. At the same time there was a peculiar fineness about the boy. His feet were astonishingly small and the hands thin and slender for all their supple strength. And his neck was not bony, as it is in most youths at this gawky age, but smoothly rounded.

Men grow big of bone and sparse of flesh in the mountain-desert. It was the more surprising to Pierre to see this young fellow with the marvelously delicate-cut features. By some freak of nature here was a place where the breed ran to high blood.

The cleaning completed, the boy tossed the butt of the gun to his shoulder and squinted down the barrel. Then he loaded the magazine, weighted the gun deftly at the balance, and dropped the rifle across his knees.

"Morning," said Pierre le Rouge cheerily, and swung off the bunk to the floor. "How old's the gun?"

The boy, without the slightest show of excitement, snapped the butt to his shoulder and drew a bead on Pierre's breast.

"Sit down before you get all heated up," said a musical voice. "There's nobody waiting for you on horseback."

And Pierre sat down, partly because Western men never argue a point when that little black hole is staring them in the face, partly because he remembered with a rush that the last time he had fully possessed his consciousness he had been lying in the snow with the cross gripped hard and the toppling mass of the landslide above him. All that had happened between was blotted from his memory. He fumbled at his throat. The cross was not there. He touched his pockets.

"Ease your hands away from your hip," said the cold voice of the boy, who had dropped his gun to the ready with a significant finger curled around the trigger, "or I'll drill you clean."

Pierre obediently raised his hands to the level of his shoulders. The boy sneered.

"This isn't a hold-up," he explained. "Put 'em down again, but watch yourself."

The sneer varied to a contemptuous smile.

"I guess you're tame, all right."

"Point that gun another way, will you, son?"

The boy flushed.

"Don't call me son."

"Is this a lockup—a jail?"

"This?"

"What is it, then? The last I remember I was lying in the snow with—"

"I wish to God you'd been let there," said the boy bitterly.

But Pierre, overwhelmed with the endeavor to recollect, rushed on with his questions and paid no heed to the tone.

"I had a cross in my hand—"

The scorn of the boy grew to mighty proportions.

"It's there in the breast-pocket of your shirt."

Pierre drew out the little cross, and the touch of it against his palm restored whatever of his strength was lacking. Very carefully he attached it to the chain about his throat. Then he looked up to the contempt of the boy, and as he did so another memory burst on him and brought him to his feet. The gun went to the boy's shoulders at the same time.

"When I was found—was anyone else with me?"

"Nope."

"What happened?"

"Must have been buried in the landslide. Half a hill

caved in, and the dirt rolled you down to the bottom. Plain luck, that's all, that kept you from going out."

"Luck?" said Pierre and he laid his hand against his breast where he could feel the outline of the cross. "Yes, I suppose it was luck. And she—"

He sat down slowly and buried his face in his hands. A new tone came in the voice of the boy as he asked: "Was a woman with you?" But Pierre heard only the tone and not the words. His face was gray when he looked up again, and his voice hard.

"Tell me as briefly as you can how I come here, and who picked me up."

"My father and his men. They passed you lying on the snow. They brought you home."

"Who is your father?"

The boy stiffened and his color rose.

"My father is Jim Boone."

Instinctively, while he stared, the right hand of Pierre le Rouge crept toward his hip.

"Keep your hand steady," said the boy. "I got a nervous trigger-finger. Yeh, dad is pretty well known."

"You're his son?"

"I'm Jack Boone."

"But I've heard—tell me, why am I under guard?"

Jack was instantly aflame with the old anger.

"Not because I want you here."

"Who does?"

"Dad."

"Put away your pop-gun and talk sense. I won't try to get away until Jim Boone comes. I only fight men."

Even the anger and grief of the boy could not keep him from smiling.

"Just the same I'll keep the shooting-iron handy. Sit still. A gun don't keep me from talking sense, does it? You're here to take Hal's place. Hal!"

The little wail told a thousand things, and Pierre, shocked out of the thought of his own troubles, waited.

"My brother, Hal; he's dead; he died last night, and on the way back dad found you and brought you to take Hal's place. *Hal's* place!"

The accent showed how impossible it was that Hal's place could be taken by any mortal man.

"I got orders to keep you here, but if I was to do what I'd like to do, I'd give you the best horse on the place and tell you to clear out. That's me!"

"Then do it."

"And face dad afterward?"

"Tell him I overpowered you. That would be easy; you a slip of a boy, and me a man."

"Stranger, it goes to show you may have heard of Jim Boone, but you don't anyways know him. When he orders a thing done he wants it done, and he don't care how, and he don't ask questions why. He just raises hell."

"He really expects to keep me here?"

"Expects? He will."

"Going to tie me up?" asked Pierre ironically.

"Maybe," answered Jack, overlooking the irony. "Maybe he'll just put you on my shoulders to guard."

He moved the gun significantly.

"And I can do it."

"Of course. But he would have to let me go sometime."

"Not till you'd promised to stick by him. I told him that myself, but he said that you're young and that he'd teach you to like this life whether you wanted to or not. Me speaking personally, I agree with Black Gandil: This is the worst fool thing that dad has ever done. What do we want with you—in Hal's place!"

"But I've got a thing to do right away—today; it can't wait."

"Give dad your word to come back and he'll let you go. He says you're the kind that will keep your word. You see,

52

he found you with a cross in your hand."

And Jack's lips curled again.

It was all absurd, too impossible to be real. The only real things were the body of yellow-haired Mary Brown, under the tumbled rocks and dirt of the landslide, and the body of Martin Ryder waiting to be placed in that corner plot where the grass grew quicker than all other grass in the spring of the year.

However, having fallen among madmen, he must use cunning to get away before the outlaw and his men came back from wherever they had gone. Otherwise there would be more bloodshed, more play of guns and hum of lead.

"Tell me of Hal," he said, and dropped his elbows on his knees as if he accepted his fate.

"Don't know you well enough to talk of Hal."

"I'm sorry."

The boy made a little gesture of apology.

"I guess that was a mean thing to say. Sure I'll tell you about Hal—if I can."

"Tell me anything you can," said Pierre gently, "because I've got to try to be like him, haven't I?"

"You could try till rattlers got tame, but it'd take ten like you to make one like Hal. He was dad's own son—he was my brother."

The sob came openly now, and the tears were a mist in the boy's eyes.

"What's your name?"

"Pierre."

"Pierre? I suppose I got to learn it."

"I suppose so." And he edged farther forward so that he was sitting only on the edge of the bunk.

"Please do." And he gathered his feet under him, ready for a spring forward and a grip at the boy's threatening rifle.

Jack had canted his head a little to one side.

"Did you ever see a horse that was gentle and yet had never been ridden, or his spirit broke, Pierre—"

Here Pierre made his leap swift as some bobcat of the northern woods; his hand whipped out as lightning fast as the striking paw of the lynx, and the gun was jerked from the hands of Jack. Not before the boy clutched at it with a cry of horror, but the force of the pull sent him lurching to the floor and broke his grip.

He was up in an instant, however, and a knife of ugly length glittered in his hand as he sprang at Pierre.

Pierre tossed aside the rifle and met the attack bare-handed. He caught the knife-bearing hand at the wrist and under his grip the hand loosened its hold and the steel tinkled on the floor. His other arm caught the body of Jack in a mighty vise.

There was a brief and futile struggle, and a hissing of breath in the silence till the hat tumbled from the head of Jack and down over the shoulders streamed a torrent of silken black hair.

Pierre stepped back. This was the meaning, then, of the strangely small feet and hands and the low music of the voice. It was the body of a girl that he had held.

11

It was not fear nor shame that made the eyes of Jacqueline so wide as she stared past Pierre toward the door. He glanced across his shoulder, and blocking the entrance to the room, literally filling the doorway, was the bulk of Jim Boone.

"Seems as if I was sort of steppin' in on a little family party," he said. "I'm sure glad you two got acquainted so quick. Jack, how did you and— What the hell's your name, lad?"

"He tricked me, dad, or he would never have got the gun away from me. This—this Pierre—this beast—he got me to talk of Hal. Then he stole—"

"The point," said Jim Boone coldly, "is that he *got* the gun. Run along, Jack. You ain't so growed up as I was thinkin'. Or hold on—maybe you're *more* grown up. Which is it? Are you turnin' into a woman, Jack?"

She whirled on Pierre in a white fury.

"You see? You see what you've done? He'll never trust me again—never! Pierre, I hate you. I'll always hate you. And if Hal were here—"

A storm of sobs and tears cut her short, and she disappeared through the door. Boone and Pierre stood regarding each other critically.

Pierre spoke first: "You're not as big as I expected."

"I'm plenty big; but you're older than I thought."

"Too old for what you want of me. The girl told me what that was."

"Not too old to be made what I want."

And his hands passed through a significant gesture of molding the empty air. The boy met his eye dauntlessly.

"I suppose," he said, "that I've a pretty small chance of getting away."

"Just about none, Pierre. Come here."

Pierre stepped closer and looked down the hall into another room. There, about a table, sat the five grimmest riders of the mountain-desert that he had ever seen. They were such men as one could judge at a glance, and Pierre made that instinctive motion for his six-gun.

"The girl," Jim Boone was saying, "kept you pretty busy tryin' to make a break, and if she could do anything maybe you'd have a pile of trouble with one of them guardin' you. But if I'd had a good look at you, lad, I'd never have let Jack take the job of guardin' you."

"Thanks," answered Pierre dryly.

"You got reason; I can see that. Here's the point, Pierre. I know young men because I can remember pretty close what I was at your age. I wasn't any ladies' lap dog, at that, but time and older men molded me the way I'm going to mold you. Understand?"

Pierre was nerved for many things, but the last word made him stir. It roused in him a red-tinged desire to get through the forest of black beard at the throat of Boone and dim the glitter of those keen eyes. It brought him also another thought.

Two great tasks lay before him: the burial of his father and the avenging of him on McGurk. As to the one, he knew it would be childish madness for him to attempt to bury his father in Morgantown with only his single hand to hold back the powers of the law or the friends of the notorious Diaz and crippled Hurley.

And for the other, it was even more vain to imagine that through his own unaided power he could strike down a figure of such almost legendary terror as McGurk. The bondage of the gang might be a terrible thing through the future, but the present need blinded him to what might come.

He said: "Suppose I stop raising questions or making a fight, but give you my hand and call myself a member—"

"Of the family? Exactly. If you did that I'd know it was because you were wantin' something, Pierre, eh?"

"Two things."

"Lad, I like this way of talk. One—two—you hit quick like a two-gun man. Well, I'm used to paying high for what I get. What's up?"

"The first—"

"Wait. Can I help you out by myself, or do you need the gang?"

"The gang."

"Then come, and I'll put it up to them. You first."

It was equally courtesy and caution, and Pierre smiled faintly as he went first through the door. He stood in a moment under the eyes of five silent men.

The booming voice of Jim Boone pronounced: "This is Pierre. He'll be one of us if he can get the gang to do two things. I ask you, will you hear him for me, and then pass on whether or not you try his game?"

They nodded. There were no greetings to acknowledge the introduction. They waited, eyeing the youth with distrust.

Pierre eyed them in turn, and then he spoke directly to big Dick Wilbur.

"Here's the first: I want to bury a man in Morgantown and I need help to do it."

Black Gandil snarled: "You heard me, boys; blood to start with. Who's the man you want us to put out?"

"He's dead—my father."

They came up straight in their chairs like trained actors rising to a stage crisis. The snarl straightened on the lips of Black Morgan Gandil.

"He's lying in his house a few miles out of Morgantown. As he died he told me that he wanted to be buried in a corner plot in the Morgantown graveyard. He'd seen the place and counted it for his a good many years because he said the grass grew quicker there than any other place, after the snow went."

"A damned good reason," said Garry Patterson. As the idea stuck more deeply into his imagination he smashed his fist down on the table so that the crockery on it danced. "A damned good reason, say I!"

"Who's your father?" asked Dick Wilbur, who eyed

57

Pierre more critically but with less enmity than the rest.

"Martin Ryder."

"A ringer!" cried Bud Mansie, and he leaned forward alertly. "You remember what I said, Jim?"

"Shut up. Pierre, talk soft and talk quick. We all know Mart Ryder had only two sons and you're not either of them."

The Northerner grew stiff and as his face grew pale the red mark where the stone had struck his forehead stood out like a danger signal.

He said slowly: "I'm his son, but not by the mother of those two."

"Was he married twice?"

Pierre was paler still, and there was an uneasy twitching of his right hand which every man understood.

He barely whispered. "No; damn you!"

But Black Gandil loved evil.

He said, with a marvelously unpleasant smile: "Then she was—"

The voice of Dick Wilbur cut in like the snapping of a whip: "Shut up, Gandil, you devil!"

There were times when not even Boone would cross Wilbur, and this was one of them.

Pierre went on: "The reason I can't go to Morgantown is that I'm not very well liked by some of the men there."

"Why not?"

"When my father died there was no money to pay for his burial. I had only a half-dollar piece. I went to the town and gambled and won a great deal. But before I came out I got mixed up with a man called Hurley, a professional gambler."

"And Diaz?" queried a chorus.

"Yes. Hurley was hurt in the wrist and Diaz died. I think I'm wanted in Morgantown."

Out of a little silence came the voice of Black Gandil:

"Dick, I'm thankin' you now for cuttin' me so short a minute ago."

Phil Branch had not spoken, as usual, but now he repeated, with rapt, far-off eyes: "'Hurley was hurt in the wrist and Diaz died?' Hurley and Diaz! I played with Hurley, a couple of times."

"Speakin' personal," said Garry Patterson, his red verging toward purple in excitement, "which I'm ready to go with you down to Morgantown and bury your father."

"And do it shipshape," added Black Gandil.

"With all the trimmings," said Bud Mansie, "with all Morgantown joinin' the mournin' voluntarily under cover of our six-guns."

"Wait," said Boone. "What's the second request?"

"That can wait."

"It's a bigger job than this one?"

"Lots bigger."

"And in the meantime?"

"I'm your man."

They shook hands. Even Black Gandil rose to take his share in the ceremony—all save Bud Mansie, who had glanced out the window a moment before and then silently left the room. A bottle of whisky was produced and glasses filled all round. Jim Boone brought in the seventh chair and placed it at the table. They raised their glasses.

"To the empty chair," said Boone.

They drank, and for the first time in his life, the liquid fire went down the throat of Pierre. He set down his glass, coughing, and the others laughed good-naturedly.

"Started down the wrong way?" asked Wilbur.

"It's beastly stuff; first I ever drank."

A roar of laughter answered him.

"Still I got an idea," broke in Jim Boone, "that he's worthy of takin' the seventh chair. Draw it up lad."

Vaguely it reminded Pierre of a scene in some old play

with himself in the role of the hero signing away his soul to the devil, but an interruption kept him from taking the chair. There was a racket at the door—a half-sobbing, half-scolding voice, and the laughter of a man; then Bud Mansie appeared carrying Jack in spite of her struggles. He placed her on the floor and held her hands to protect himself from her fury.

"I glimpsed her through the window," he explained. "She was lining out for the stable and then a minute later I saw her swing a saddle onto—what horse d'you think?"

"Out with it."

"Jim's big Thunder. Yep, she stuck the saddle on big black Thunder and had a rifle in the holster. I saw there was hell brewing somewhere, so I went out and nabbed her."

"Jack!" called Jim Boone. "What were you started for?"

Bud Mansie released her arms and she stood with them stiffening at her sides and her fists clenched.

"Hal—he died, and there was nothing but talk about him—nothing done. You got a live man in Hal's place."

She pointed an accusing finger at Pierre.

"Maybe he takes his place for you, but he's not my brother—I hate him. I went out to get another man to make up for Pierre."

"Well?"

"A dead man. I shoot straight enough for that."

A very solemn silence spread through the room; for every man was watching in the eyes of the father and daughter the same shining black devil of wrath.

"Jack, get into your room and don't move out of it till I tell you to. D'you hear?"

She turned on her heel like a soldier and marched from the room.

"Jack."

She stopped in the door but would not turn back.

"Jack, don't you love your old dad anymore?"

She whirled and ran to him with outstretched arms and clung to him, sobbing.

"Oh, dad," she groaned. "You've broken my heart."

12

The annals of the mountain-desert have never been written and can never be written. They are merely a vast mass of fact and tradition and imagining which floats from tongue to tongue from the Rockies to the Sierra Nevadas. A man may be a fact all his life and die only a local celebrity. Then again, he may strike sparks from that imagination which runs riot by camp-fires and at the bars of the crossroads saloons.

In that case he becomes immortal. It is not that lies are told about him or impossible feats ascribed to him, but every detail about him is seized upon and passed on with a most scrupulous and loving care.

In due time he will become a tradition. That is, he will be known familiarly at widely separated parts of the range, places which he has never visited. It has happened to a few of the famous characters of the mountain-desert that they became traditions before their deaths. It happened to McGurk, of course. It also happened to Red Pierre.

Oddly enough, the tradition of Red Pierre did not begin with his ride from the school of Father Victor to Morgantown, distant many days of difficult and dangerous travel. Neither did tradition seize on the gunfight that crippled Hurley and "put out" wizard Diaz. These things were unquestionably known to many, but they did not strike the popular imagination. What set men first on fire was the way Pierre le Rouge buried his father "at the point of the gun" in Morgantown.

That day Boone's men galloped out of the higher mountains down the trail toward Morgantown. They stole a wagon out of a ranch stable on the way and tied two lariats to the tongue. So they towed it, bounding and rattling, over the rough trail to the house where Martin Ryder lay dead.

His body was placed in state in the body of the wagon, pillowed with everything in the line of cloth which the house could furnish. Thus equipped they went on at a more moderate pace toward Morgantown.

What followed it is useless to repeat here. Tradition rehearsed every detail of that day's work, and the purpose of this narrative is only to give the details of some of the events which tradition does not know, at least in their entirety.

They started at one end of Morgantown's street. Pierre guarded the wagon in the center of the street and kept the people under cover of his rifle. The rest of Boone's men cleaned out the houses as they went and sent the occupants piling out to swell the crowd.

And so they rolled the crowd out of town and to the cemetery, where "volunteers" dug the grave of Martin Ryder wide and deep, and Pierre paid for the corner plot three times over in gold.

Then a coffin—improvised hastily for the occasion out of a packing-box—was lowered reverently, also by "volunteer" mourners, and before the first sod fell on the dead. Pierre raised over his head the crucifix of Father Victor that brought good luck, and intoned a service in the purest

Ciceronian Latin, surely, that ever regaled the ears of Morgantown's elect.

The moment he raised that cross the bull throat of Jim Boone bellowed a command, the poised guns of the gang enforced it, and all the crowd dropped to their knees, leaving the six outlaws scattered about the edges of the mob like sheep dogs around a folding flock, while in the center stood Pierre with white, upturned face and the raised cross.

So Martin Ryder was buried with "trimmings," and the gang rode back, laughing and shouting, through the town and up into the safety of the mountains. Election day was fast approaching and therefore the rival candidates for sheriff hastily organized posses and made the usual futile pursuit.

In fact, before the pursuit was well under way, Boone and his men sat at their supper table in the cabin. The seventh chair was filled; all were present except Jack, who sulked in her room. Pierre went to her door and knocked. He carried under his arm a package which he had secured in the General Merchandise Store of Morgantown.

"We're all waiting for you at the table," he explained.

"Just keep on waiting," said the husky voice of Jacqueline.

"I've brought you a present."

"I hate your presents!"

"It's a thing you've wanted for a long time, Jacqueline."
Only a stubborn silence.

"I'm putting your door a little ajar."

"If you dare to come in I'll—"

"And I'm leaving the package right here at the entrance. I'm so sorry, Jacqueline, that you hate me."

And then he walked off down the hall—cunning Pierre—before she could send her answer like an arrow after him. At the table he arranged an eighth plate and drew up a chair before it.

"If that's for Jack," remarked Dick Wilbur, "you're wasting your time. I know her and I know her type. She'll never come out to the table tonight—nor tomorrow, either. I know!"

In fact, he knew a good deal too much about girls and women also, did Wilbur, and that was why he rode the long trails of the mountain-desert with Boone and his men. Far south and east in the Bahamas a great mansion stood vacant because he was gone, and the dust lay thick on the carpets and powdered the curtains and tapestries with a common gray.

He had built it and furnished it for a woman he loved, and afterward for her sake he had killed a man and fled from a posse and escaped in the steerage of a west-bound ship. Still the law followed him, and he kept on west and west until he reached the mountain-desert, which thinks nothing of swallowing men and their reputations.

There he was safe, but someday he would see some woman smile, catch the glimmer of some eye, and throw safety away to ride after her.

It was a weakness, but what made a tragic figure of handsome Dick Wilbur was that he knew his weakness and sat still and let fate walk up and overtake him.

Yet Pierre le Rouge answered this man of sorrowful wisdom: "In my part of the country men say: 'If you would speak of women let money talk for you.'"

And he placed a gold piece on the table.

"She will come out to the supper table."

"She will not," smiled Wilbur, and covered the coin. "Will you take odds?"

"No charity. Who else will bet?"

"I," said Jim Boone instantly. "You figure her for an ordinary sulky kid."

Pierre smiled upon him.

"There's a cut in my shirt where her knife passed through; and that's the reason that I'll bet on her now."

The whole table covered his coin, with laughter.

"We've kept one part of your bargain, Pierre. We've seen your father buried in the corner plot. Now, what's the second part?"

"I don't know you well enough to ask you that," said Pierre.

They plied him with suggestions.

"To rob the Berwin Bank?"

"Stick up a train?"

"No. That's nothing."

"Round up the sheriffs from here to the end of the mountains?"

"Too easy."

"Roll all those together," said Pierre, "and you'll begin to get an idea of what I'll ask."

Then a low voice called from the black throat of the hall: "Pierre!"

The others were silent, but Pierre winked at them, and made great flourish with knife and fork against his plate as if to cover the sound of Jacqueline's voice.

"Pierre!" she called again. "I've come to thank you."

He jumped up and turned toward the hall.

"Do you like it?"

"It's a wonder!"

"Then we're friends?"

"If you want to be."

"There's nothing I want more. Then you'll come out and have supper with us, Jack?"

There was a little pause, and then Jim Boone struck his fist on the table and cursed, for she stepped from the darkness into the flaring light of the room.

13

She wore a cartridge-belt slung jauntily across her hips and from it hung a holster of stiff new leather with the top flap open to show the butt of a man-sized forty-five caliber six-shooter—her first gun. Not a man of the gang but had loaned her his guns time and again, but they had never dreamed of giving her a weapon of her own.

So they stared at her agape, where she stood with her head back, one hand resting on her hip, one hovering about the butt of the gun, as if she challenged them to question her right to be called "man."

It was as if she abandoned all claims to femininity with that single step; the gun at her side made her seem inches taller and years older. She was no longer a child, but a long-rider who could shoot with the best.

One glance she cast about the room to drink in the amazement of the gang, and then her father broke in rather hoarsely: "Sit down, girl. Sit down and be one of us. One of us you are by your own choice from this day on. You're neither man nor woman, but a long-rider with every man's hand against you. You've done with any hope of a home or of friends. You're one of us. Poor Jack—my girl!"

"Poor?" she returned. "Not while I can make a quick draw and shoot straight."

And then she swept the circle of eyes, daring them to take her boast lightly, but they knew her too well, and were all solemnly silent. At this she relented somewhat, and went directly to Pierre, flushing from throat to hair. She held out her hand.

"Will you shake and call it square?"

"I sure will," nodded Pierre.

"And we're pals—you and me, like the rest of 'em?"

"We are."

She took the place beside him.

As the whisky went round after round the two seemed shut away from the others; they were younger, less marked by life; they listened while the others talked, and now and then exchanged glances of interest or aversion.

"Listen," she said after a time, "I've heard this story before."

It was Phil Branch, square-built and square of jaw, who was talking.

"There's only one thing I can handle better than a gun, and that's a sledgehammer. A gun is all right in its way, but for work in a crowd, well, give me a hammer and I'll show you a way out."

Bud Mansie grinned: "Leave me my pair of sixes and you can have all the hammers between here and Central Park in a crowd. There's nothing makes a crowd remember its heels like a pair of barking sixes."

"Ah, ah!" growled Branch. "But when they've heard bone crunch under the hammer there's nothing will hold them."

"I'd have to see that."

"Maybe you will, Bud, maybe you will. It was the hammer that started me for the trail west. I had a big Scotchman in the factory who couldn't learn how to weld. I'd taught him day after day and cursed him and damn near prayed for him. But he somehow wouldn't learn—the swine—ah, ah!"

He grew vindictively black at the memory.

"Every night he wiped out what I'd taught him during

the day and the eraser he used was booze. So one fine day I dropped the hammer after watchin' him make a botch on a big bar, and cussed him up one leg and down the other. The Scotchman had a hangover from the night before and he made a pass at me. It was too much for me just then, for the day was hot and the forge fire had been spitting cinders in my face all morning. So I took him by the throat."

He reached out and closed his taut fingers slowly.

"I didn't mean nothin' by it, but after a man has been moldin' iron, flesh is pretty weak stuff. When I let go of Scotchy he dropped on the floor, and while I stood starin' down at him somebody seen what had happened and spread the word.

"I wasn't none too popular, bein' not much on talk, so the boys got together and pretty soon they come pilin' through the door at me, packin' everything from hatchets to crowbars.

"Lads, I was sorry about Scotchy, but after I glimpsed that gang comin' I wasn't sorry for nothing. I felt like singin', though there wasn't no song that could say just what I meant. But I grabbed up the big fourteen-pound hammer and met 'em halfway.

"The first swing of the hammer it met something hard, but not as hard as iron. The thing crunched with a sound like an egg under a man's heel. And when that crowd heard it they looked sick. God, how sick they looked! They didn't wait for no second swing, but they beat it hard and fast through the door with me after 'em. They scattered, but I kept right on and didn't never really stop till I reached the mountain-desert and you, Jim."

"Which is a good yarn," said Bud Mansie, "but I can tell you one that'll cap it. It was—"

He stopped short, staring up at the door. Outside, the wind had kept up a perpetual roaring, and no one noticed the noise of the opening door. Bud Mansie, facing that door, however, turned a queer yellow and sat with his lips parted on the last word. He was not pretty to see. The others turned their heads, and there followed the strangest panic which Pierre had ever seen.

Jim Boone jerked his hand back to his hip, but stayed the motion, half completed, and swung his hands stiffly above his head. Garry Patterson sat with his eyes blinked shut, pale, waiting for death to come. Dick Wilbur rose, tall and stiff, and stood with his hands gripped at his sides, and Black Morgan Gandil clutched at the table before him and his eyes wandered swiftly about the room, seeking a place for escape.

There was only one sound, and that was a whispering moan of terror from Jacqueline. Only Pierre made no move, yet he felt as he had when the black mass of the landslide loomed above him.

What he saw in the door was a man of medium size and almost slender build. In spite of the patch of gray hair at either temple he was only somewhere between twenty-five and thirty. But to see him was to forget all details except the strangest face which Pierre had ever seen or would ever look upon in all his career.

It was pale, with a pallor strange to the ranges; even the lips seemed bloodless, and they curved with a suggestion of a smile that was a nervous habit rather than any sign of mirth. The nerves of the left eye were also affected, and the lid dropped and fluttered almost shut, so that he had to carry his head far back in order to see plainly. There was such pride and scorn in the man that his name came up to the lips of Pierre: "McGurk."

A surprisingly gentle voice said: "Jim, I'm sorry to drop in on you this way, but I've had some unpleasant news."

His words dispelled part of the charm. The hands of big Boone lowered; the others assumed more natural positions, but each, it seemed to Pierre, took particular and almost ostentatious care that their right hands should be always far from the holsters of their guns.

The stranger went on: "Martin Ryder is finished, as I suppose you know. He left a spawn of two mongrels behind him. I haven't bothered with them, but I'm a little more interested in another son that has cropped up. He's sitting over there in your family party and his name is Pierre. In his own country they call him Pierre le Rouge, which means Red Pierre, in our talk.

"You know I've never crossed you in anything before, Jim. Have I?"

Boone moistened his white lips and answered: "Never," huskily, as if it were a great muscular effort for him to speak.

"This time I have to break the custom. Boone, this fellow Pierre has to leave the country. Will you see that he goes?"

The lips of Boone moved and made no sound.

He said at length: "McGurk, I'd rather cross the devil than cross you. There's no shame in admitting that. But I've lost my boy, Hal."

"Too bad, Jim. I knew Hal; at a distance, of course."

"And Pierre is filling Hal's place in the family."

"Is that your answer?"

"McGurk, are you going to pin me down in this?"

And here Jack whirled and cried: "Dad, you won't let Pierre go!"

"You see?" pleaded Boone.

It was uncanny and horrible to see the giant so unnerved before this stranger, but that part of it did not come to Pierre until later. Now he felt a peculiar emptiness of stomach and a certain jumping chill that traveled up and down his spine. Moreover, he could not move his eyes from the face of McGurk, and he knew at length that this was fear—the first real fear that he had ever known.

Shame made him hot, but fear made him cold again. He

knew that if he rose his knees would buckle under him; that if he drew out his revolver it would slip from his palsied fingers. For the fear of death is a mighty fear, but it is nothing compared with the fear of man.

"I've asked you a question," said McGurk. "What's your answer?"

There was a quiver in the black forest of Boone's beard, and if Pierre was cold before, he was sick at heart to see the big man cringe before McGurk.

He stammered: "Give me time."

"Good," said McGurk. "I'm afraid I know what your answer would be now, but if you take a couple of days you will think things over and come to a reasonable conclusion. I will be at Gaffney's place about fifteen miles from here. You know it? Send your answer there. In the meantime"— he stepped forward to the table and poured a small drink of whisky into a glass and raised it high—"here's to the long health and happiness of us all. Drink!"

There was a hasty pouring of liquor.

"And you also!"

Pierre jumped as if he had been struck, and obeyed the order hastily.

"So," said the master, pleasant again, and Pierre wiped his forehead furtively and stared up with fascinated eyes. "An unwilling pledge is better than none at all. To you, gentlemen, much happiness; to you, Pierre le Rouge, *bon voyage*."

They drank; the master placed his glass on the table again, smiled upon them, and was gone through the door. He turned his back in leaving. There was no fitter way in which he could have expressed his contempt.

14

The mirth died and in its place came a long silence. Jim Boone stared upon Pierre with miserable eyes, and then rose and left the room. The others one by one followed his example. Dick Wilbur in passing dropped his hand on Pierre's shoulder. Jacqueline was silent.

As he sat there minute after minute and then hour after hour of the long night Pierre saw the meaning of it. If they sent word that they would not give up Pierre it was war, and war with McGurk had only one ending. If they sent word that Pierre was surrendered the shame would never leave Boone and his men.

Whatever they did there was ruin for them in the end. All this Pierre conned slowly in his mind, until he was cold. Then he looked up and saw that the lamp had burned out and that the wood in the fireplace was consumed to a few red embers.

He replenished the fire, and when the yellow flames began to mount he made his resolution and walked slowly up and down the floor with it. For he knew that he must go to meet McGurk.

The very thought of the man sent the old chill through his blood, yet he must go and face him and end the thing.

It came over him with a pang that he was very young; that life was barely a taste in his mouth, whether bitter or sweet he could not tell. He picked a flaming stick from the fire and went before a little round mirror on the wall.

Back at him stared the face of a boy. He had seen so

much of the grim six in the last day that the contrast startled him. They were men, hardened to life and filled with knowledge of it. They were books written full. But he? He was a blank page with a scribbled word here and there. Nevertheless, he was chosen and he must go.

Having reached that decision he closed his mind on what would happen. There was a vague fear that when he faced McGurk he would be frozen with fear; that his spirit would be broken and he would become a thing too despicable for a man to kill.

One thing was certain: if he was to act a man's part and die a man's death he must not stand long before McGurk. It seemed to him then that he would die happy if he had the strength to fire one shot before the end.

Then he tiptoed from the house and went over the snow to the barn and saddled the horse of Hal Boone. It was already morning, and as he led the horse to the door of the barn a shadow, a faint shadow in that early light, fell across the snow before him.

He looked up and saw Jacqueline. She stepped close, and the horse nosed her shoulder affectionately.

She said: "Isn't there anything that will keep you from going?"

"It's just a little ride before breakfast. I'll be back in an hour."

It was foolish to try to blind her, as he saw by her wan, unchildish smile.

"Is there no other way, Pierre?"

"I don't know of any, do you?"

"You have to leave us, and never come back?"

"Is he as sure as that, Jack?"

"Sure? Who?"

She had not known, after all; she thought that he was merely riding away from the region where McGurk was king. Now she caught his wrists and shook them.

"Pierre, you are not going to face McGurk? Pierre!"

"If you were a man, you would understand."

"I know; because of your father. I *do* understand, but oh, Pierre, listen! I can shoot as straight as almost any man. We will ride down together. We will go through the doors together—me first to take his fire, and you behind to shoot him down."

"I guess no man can be as brave as a woman, Jack. No; I have to see McGurk alone. He faced my father alone and shot him down. I'll face McGurk alone and live long enough to put my mark on him."

"But you don't know him. He can't be hurt. Do you think my father and—and Dick Wilbur would fear any man who could be hurt? No, but McGurk has been in a hundred fights and never been touched. There's a charm over him, don't you see?"

"I'll break the charm, that's all."

He was up in the saddle.

"Then I'll call dad—I'll call them all—if you die they shall all follow you. I swear they shall. Pierre!"

He merely leaned forward and touched the horse with his spurs, but after he had raced the first hundred yards he glanced back. She was running hard for the house, and calling as she went. Pierre cursed and spurred the horse again.

Yet even if Jim Boone and his men started out after him they could never overtake him. Before they were in their saddles and up with him, he'd be a full three miles out in the hills. Not even black Thunder could make up as much ground as that.

So all the fifteen miles to Gaffney's place he urged his horse. The excitement of the race kept the thought of McGurk back in his mind. Only once he lost time when he had to pull up beside a buckboard and inquire the way. After that he flew on again. Yet as he clattered up to the door of Gaffney's crossroads saloon and swung to the ground he looked back and saw a cluster of horsemen swing around the shoulder of a hill and come tearing after him. Surely his time was short.

He thrust open the door of the place and called for a drink. The bartender spun the glass down the bar to him.

"Where's McGurk?"

The other stopped in the very act of taking out the bottle from the shelf, and his curious glance went over the face of Pierre le Rouge. He decided, apparently, that it was foolish to hold suspicions against so young a man.

"In that room," and he jerked his hand toward a door. "What do you want with him?"

"Got a message for him."

"Tell it to me, and I'll pass it along."

Pierre met the eye of the other and smiled faintly.

"Not *this* message."

"Oh," said the other, and then shouted: "McGurk!"

Far away came the rush of hoofs over a hard trail. Only a minute more and they would be here; only a minute more and the room would be full of fighting men ready to die with him and for him. Yet Pierre was glad; glad that he could meet the danger alone; ten minutes from now, if he lived, he could answer certainly one way or the other the greatest of all questions: "Am I a man?"

Out of the inner room the pleasant voice which he dreaded answered: "What's up?"

The barkeeper glanced Pierre le Rouge over again and then answered: "A friend with a message."

The door opened and framed McGurk. He did not start, seeing Pierre.

He said: "None of the rest of them had the guts even to bring me the message, eh?"

Pierre shrugged his shoulders. It was a mighty effort, but he was able to look his man fairly in the eyes.

"All right, lad. How long is it going to take you to clear out of the country?"

"That's not the message," answered a voice which Pierre did not recognize as his own.

"Out with it, then."

"It's in the leather on my hip."

And he went for his gun. Even as he started his hand he knew that he was too slow for McGurk, yet the finest split-second watch in the world could not have caught the differing time they needed to get their guns out of the holsters.

Just a breath before Pierre fired there was a stunning blow on his right shoulder and another on his hip. He lurched to the floor, his revolver clattering against the wood as he fell, but falling, he scooped up the gun with his left and twisted.

That movement made the third shot of McGurk fly wide and Pierre fired from the floor and saw a spasm of pain contract the face of the outlaw.

Instantly the door behind him flew open and Boone's men stormed into the room. Once more McGurk fired, but his wound made his aim wide and the bullet merely tore up a splinter beside Pierre's head. A fusillade from Boone and his men answered, but the outlaw had leaped back through the door.

"He's hurt," thundered Boone. "By God, the charm of McGurk is broken. Dick, Bud, Gandil, take the outside of the place. I'll force the door."

Wilbur and the other two raced through the door and raised a shout at once, and then there was a rattle of shots. Big Patterson leaned over Pierre.

He said in an awe-stricken voice: "Lad, it's a great work that you've done for all of us, if you've drawn the blood from McGurk."

"His left shoulder," said Pierre, and smiled in spite of his pain.

"And you, lad?"

"I'm going to live; I've got to finish the job. Who's that beside you? There's a mist over my eyes."

"It's Jack. She outrode us all."

Then the mist closed over the eyes of Pierre and his senses went out in the dark.

15

Those who are curious about the period which followed during which the title "Le Rouge" was forgotten and he became known only as "Red" Pierre through all the mountain-desert, can hear the tales of his doing from the analysts of the ranges. This story has to do only with his struggle with McGurk.

The gap of six years which occurs here is due to the fact that during that period McGurk vanished from the mountain-desert. He died away from the eyes of men and in their minds he became that tradition which lives still so vividly, the tradition of the pale face, the sneering, blood-less lips, and the hand which never failed.

During this lapse of time there were many who claimed that he had ridden off into some lonely haunt and died of the wound which he received from Pierre's bullet. A great majority, however, would never accept such a story, and even when the six years had rolled by they still shook their heads.

They awaited his return just as certain stanch old Britons await the second coming of Arthur from the island of Avalon. In the meantime the terror of his name passed on to him who had broken the "charm" of McGurk.

Not all that grim significance passed on to Red Pierre, indeed, because he never impressed the public imagination as did the terrible ruthlessness of McGurk. At that he did enough to keep tongues wagging.

Cattlemen loved to tell those familiar exploits of the "two sheriffs," or that "thousand-mile pursuit of Canby," with its half-tragic, half-humorous conclusion, or the "Sacking of Two Rivers," or the "three-cornered battle" against Rodriguez and Blond.

But men could not forget that in all his work there rode behind Red Pierre six dauntless warriors of the mountain-desert, while McGurk had been always a single hand against the world, a veritable lone wolf.

Whatever kept him away through those six years, the memory of the wound he received at Gaffney's place never left McGurk, and now he was coming back with a single great purpose in his mind, and in his heart a consuming hatred for Pierre and all the other of Boone's men.

Certainly if he had sensed the second coming of McGurk, Pierre would not have ridden so jauntily through the hills this day, or whistled so carelessly, or swept the hills with such a complacent, lordly eye. A man of mark cannot bear himself too modestly, and Pierre, from boots to high-peaked, broad-brimmed sombrero, was the last word in elegance for a rider of the mountain-desert.

Even his mount seemed to sense the pride of his master. It was a cream-colored mustang, not one of the lump-headed, bony-hipped species common to the ranges, but one of those rare reversions to the Spanish thoroughbreds from which the Western cow-pony is descended. The mare was not over-large, but the broad hips and generous expanse of chest were hints, and only hints, of her strength and endurance. There was the speed of the blooded racer in her and the tirelessness of the mustang.

Now, down the rocky, half-broken trail she picked her way as daintily as any debutante tiptoeing down a great stairway to the ballroom. Life had been easy for Mary since that thousand-mile struggle to overtake Canby, and now her sides were sleek from good feeding and some casual twenty miles a day, which was no more to her than a canter through the park is to the city horse.

The eye which had been so red-stained and fierce during the long ride after Canby was now bright and gentle. At every turn she pricked her small sharp ears as if she expected home and friends on the other side of the curve. And now and again she tossed her head and glanced back at the master for a moment and then whinnied across some echoing ravine.

It was Mary's way of showing happiness, and her master's acknowledgment was to run his gloved left hand up through her mane and with his ungloved right, that tanned and agile hand, pat her shoulder lightly.

Passing to the end of the down-grade, they reached a slight upward incline, and the mare, as if she had come to familiar ground, broke into a gallop, a matchless, swinging stride. Swerving to right and to left among the great boulders, like a football player running a broken field, she increased the gallop to a racing pace.

That twisting course would have shaken an ordinary horseman to the toes, but Pierre, swaying easily in the saddle, dropped the reins into the crook of his left arm and rolled a cigarette in spite of the motion and the wind. It was a little feat, but it would have drawn applause from a circus crowd.

He spoke to the mare while he lighted a match and she dropped to an easy canter, the pace which she could maintain from dawn to dark, eating up the gray miles of the mountain and the desert, and it was then that Red Pierre heard a gay voice singing in the distance.

His attitude changed at once. He caught a shorter grip on the reins and swung forward a little in the saddle, while his right hand touched the butt of the revolver in its holster and made sure that it was loose; for to those who hunt and are hunted every human voice in the mountain-desert is an ominous token.

The mare, sensing the change of her master through that weird telegraphy which passed down the taut bridle reins, held her head high and flattened her short ears against her neck.

The song and the singer drew closer, and the vigilance of Pierre ceased as he heard a mellow baritone ring out.

> "They call me poor, yet I am rich
>   In the touch of her golden hair,
> My heart is filled like a miser's hands
>   With the red-gold of her hair.
> The sky I ride beneath all day
>   Is the blue of her dear eyes;
> The only heaven I desire
>   Is the blue of her dear eyes."

And here Dick Wilbur rode about the shoulder of a hill, broke off his song at the sight of Pierre le Rouge, and shouted a welcome. They came together and continued their journey side by side. The half-dozen years had hardly altered the blond, handsome face of Wilbur, and now, with the gladness of his singing still flushing his face, he seemed hardly more than a boy—younger, in fact, than Red Pierre, into whose eyes there came now and then a grave sternness.

"After hearing that song," said Pierre smiling, "I feel as if I'd listened to a portrait."

"Right!" said Wilbur, with unabated enthusiasm. "It's the bare and unadorned truth, Prince Pierre. My fine Galahad, if you came within eye-shot of her there'd be a small-sized hell raised."

"No. I'm immune there, you know."

"Nonsense. The beauty of a really lovely woman is like a fine perfume. It strikes right to a man's heart; there's no possibility of resistance. I know. You, Pierre, act like a man already in love or a boy who has never known a woman. Which is it, Pierre?"

The other made a familiar gesture with those who knew him, a touching of his left hand against his throat where the cross lay.

He said: "I suppose it seems like that to you."

"Like what? Dodging me, eh? Well, I never press the point, but I'd give the worth of your horse, Pierre, to see you and Mary together."

Red Pierre started, and then frowned.

"Irritates you a little, eh? Well, a woman is like a spur to most men."

He added, with a momentary gloom: "God knows, I bear the marks of 'em."

He raised his head, as if he looked up in response to his thought.

"But there's a difference with this girl. I've named the quality of her before—it disarms a man."

Pierre looked to his friend with some alarm, for there was a saying among the followers of Boone that a woman would be the downfall of big Dick Wilbur again, as a woman had been his downfall before. The difference would be that this fall must be his last.

And Wilbur went on: "She's Eastern, Pierre, and out here visiting the daughter of old Barnes who owns about a thousand miles of range, you know. How long will she be here? That's the question I'm trying to answer for her. I met her riding over the hills—she was galloping along a ridge, and she rode her way right into my heart. Well, I'm a fool, of course, but about this girl I can't be wrong. Tonight I'm taking her to a masquerade."

He pulled his horse to a full stop.

"Pierre, you have to come with me."

16

Pierre stared at his companion with almost open-mouthed astonishment.

"I? A dance?"

And then his head tilted back and he laughed.

"My good times, Dick, come out of the hills and the sky-line, and the gallop of Mary. But as for women, they bore me, Dick."

"Even Jack?"

"She's more man than woman."

It was the turn of Wilbur to laugh, and he responded uproariously until Pierre frowned and flushed a little.

"When I see you out here on your horse with your rifle in the boot and your six-gun swinging low in the scabbard, and riding the fastest bit of horseflesh on the ranges," explained Wilbur, "I get to thinking that you're pretty much king of the mountains; but in certain respects, Pierre, you're a child."

Pierre stirred uneasily in his saddle. A man must be well over thirty before he can withstand ridicule.

He said dryly: "I've an idea that I know Jack's about as well as the next man."

"Let it drop," said Wilbur, sober again, for he shared with all of Boone's crew a deep-rooted unwillingness to press Red Pierre beyond a certain point. "The one subject I won't quarrel about is Jack, God bless her."

"She's the best pal," said Pierre soberly, "and the nearest to a man I've ever met."

"Nearest to a man?" queried Wilbur, and smiled, but so furtively that even the sharp eye of Red Pierre did not perceive the mockery. He went on: "But the dance, what of that? It's a masquerade. There'd be no fear of being recognized."

Pierre was silent a moment more. Then he said: "This girl—what did you call her?"

"Mary."

"And about her hair—I think you said it was black?"

"Golden, Pierre."

"Mary, and golden hair," mused Red Pierre. "I think I'll go to that dance."

"With Jack? She dances wonderfully, you know."

"Well—with Jack."

So they reached a tumbled ranch house squeezed between two hills so that it was sheltered from the storms of the winter but held all the heat of the summer.

Once it had been a goodly building, the home of some cattle king. But bad times had come.

A bullet in a saloon brawl put an end to the cattle king, and now his home was a wreck of its former glory. The northern wing shelved down to the ground as if the building were kneeling to the power of the wind, and the southern portion of the house, though still erect, seemed tottering and rotten throughout and holding together until at a final blow the whole structure would crumple at once.

To the stables, hardly less ruinous than the big house, Pierre and Wilbur took their horses, and a series of whinnies greeted them from the stalls. To look down that line of magnificent heads raised above the partitions of the stalls was like glancing into the stud of some crowned head who made hunting and racing his chief end in life, for these were animals worthy of the sport of kings.

They were chosen each from among literal hundreds, and they were cared for far more tenderly than the masters cared for themselves. There was a reason in it, for upon their speed and endurance depended the life of the outlaw. Moreover, the policy of Jim Boone was one of actual "long riding."

Here he had come to a pause for a few days to recuperate his horses and his men. Tomorrow, perhaps, he would be on the spur again and sweeping off to a distant point in the mountain-desert to strike and be gone again before the rangers knew well that he had been there. Very rarely did one settler have another neighbor at a distance of less than two hundred miles. It meant arduous and continual riding, and a horse with any defect was worse than useless because the speed of the gang had to be the speed of the slowest horse in the lot.

It was some time before the two long riders had completed the grooming of their horses and had gone down the hill and into the house. In the largest habitable room they found a fire fed with rotten timbers from the wrecked portion of the building, and scattered through the room a sullen and dejected group: Mansie, Branch, Jim Boone, and Black Morgan Gandil.

At a glance it was easy to detect their malady; it was the horrible ennui which comes to men who are always surrounded by one set of faces. If a man is happily married he may bear with his wife and his children constantly through long stretches of time, but the glamour of life lies in the varying personalities which a man glimpses in passing, but never knows.

This was a rare crew. Every man of them was marked for

courage and stamina and wild daring. Yet even so in their passive moments they hated each other with a hate that passed the understanding of common men.

Through seven years they had held together, through fair weather and foul, and now each knew from the other's expression the words that were about to be spoken, and each knew that the other was reading him, and loathing what he read.

So they were apt to relapse into long silences unless Jack was with them, for being a woman her variety was infinite, or Pierre le Rouge, whom all except Black Gandil loved and petted, and feared.

They were a battered crowd. Wind and hard weather and a thousand suns had marked them, and the hand of man had branded them. Here and there was a touch of gray in their hair, and about the mouth of each were lines which in such silent moments as this one gave an expression of yearning.

"What's up? What's wrong?" asked Wilbur from the door, but since no answer was deigned he said no more.

But Pierre, like a charmed man who dares to walk among lions, strolled easily through the room, and looked into the face of big Boone, who smiled faintly up to him, and Black Gandil, who scowled doubly dark, and Bud Mansie, who shifted uneasily in his chair and then nodded, and finally to Branch. He dropped a hand on the massive shoulder of the blacksmith.

"Well?" he asked.

Branch let himself droop back into his chair. His big, dull, colorless eyes stared up to his friend.

"I dunno, lad. I'm just weary with the sort of tired that you can't help by sleepin'. Understand?"

Pierre nodded, slowly, because he sympathized. "And the trouble?"

Branch stared about as if searching for a reason.

85

"Jack's upstairs sulking; Patterson hasn't come home yet."

And Black Gandil, who heard all things, said without looking up: "A man that saves a shipwrecked fellow, he gets bad luck for thanks."

Pierre turned a considerable eye on him, and Gandil scowled back.

"You've been croaking for six years, Morgan, about the bad luck that would come to Jim from saving me out of the snow. It's never happened, has it?"

Gandil, snarling from one side of his mouth, answered: "Where's Patterson?"

"Am I responsible if the blockhead has got drunk some-place?"

"Patterson doesn't get drunk—not that way. And he knows that we were to start again today."

"There ain't no doubt of that," commented Branch.

"It's the straight dope. Patterson keeps his dates," said Bud Mansie.

The booming bass of Jim Boone broke in: "Shut up, the whole gang of you. We've had luck for the six years Pierre has been with us. Who calls him a Jonah?"

And Black Gandil answered: "I do. I've sailed the seas. I know bad luck when I see it."

"You've been seeing it for six years."

"The worst storms come on a voyage that starts with fair weather. Patterson? He's gone; he ain't just delayed; he's gone."

It was not the first of these gloomy prophecies which Gandil had made, but each time a heavy gloom broke over Red Pierre. For when he summed up the good fortune which the cross of Father Victor had brought him, he found that he had gained a father, and lost him at their first meeting; and he had won money on that night of the gambling, but it had cost the life of another man almost at once. The horse which carried him away from the vengeance in Morgantown had died on the way and he had been saved from the landslide, but the girl had perished.

He had driven McGurk from the ranges, and where would the penalty fall on those who were near and dear to him? In a superstitious horror he had asked himself the question a thousand times, and finally he could hardly bear to look into the ominous, brooding eyes of Black Gandil. It was as if the man had a certain and evil knowledge of the future.

17

The knowledge of the torment he was inflicting made the eye of Black Gandil bright with triumph.

He continued, and now every man in the room was sitting up, alert, with gloomy eyes fixed upon Pierre: "Patterson is the first, but he ain't the last. He's just the start. Who's next?" He looked slowly around.

"Is it you, Bud, or you, Phil, or you, Jim, or maybe me?"

And Pierre said: "What makes you think you know that trouble's coming, Morgan?"

"Because my blood runs cold in me when I look at you."

Red Pierre grew rigid and straightened in a way they knew.

"Damn you, Gandil, I've borne with you and your croaking too long, d'ye hear? Too long, and I'll hear no more of it, understand?"

"Why not? You'll hear from me every time I sight you in the offing. You c'n lay to that!"

The others were tense, ready to spring for cover, but Boone reared up his great figure.

"Don't answer him, Pierre. You, Gandil, shut your face or I'll break ye in two."

The fierce eyes of Pierre le Rouge never wavered from his victim, but he answered: "Keep out of this. This is *my* party. I'll tell you why you'll stop gibbering, Gandil."

He made a pace forward and every man shrank a little away from him.

"Because the cold in your blood is part hate and more fear, Black Gandil."

The eyes of Gandil glared back for an instant. With all his soul he yearned for the courage to pull his gun, but his arm was numb; he could not move it, and his eyes wavered and fell.

The shaggy gray head of Jim Boone fell likewise, and he was murmuring to his savage old heart: "The good days are over. They'll never rest till one of 'em is dead, and then the rest will take sides and we'll have gun-plays at night. Seven years, and then to break up!"

Dick Wilbur, as usual, was the pacifier. He strode across the room, and the sharp sound of his heels on the creaking floor broke the tension. He said softly to Pierre: "You've raised hell enough. Now let's go and get Jack down here to undo what you've just finished. Besides, you've got to ask her for that dance, eh?"

The glance of Pierre still lingered on Gandil as he turned and followed Wilbur up the complaining stairs to the one habitable room in the second story of the house. It was set aside for the use of Jacqueline.

At the door Wilbur said: "Shrug your shoulders back; you look as if you were going to jump at something. And wipe the wolf look off your face. After all, Jack's a girl, not a gunfighter."

Then he knocked and opened the door.

She lay face down on her bunk, her head turned from them toward the wall. Slender and supple and strong, it was still only the size of her boots and her hands that would make one look at her twice and then guess that this was a woman, for she was dressed, from trousers even to the bright bandanna knotted around her throat, like any prosperous range rider.

Now, to be sure, the thick coils of black hair told her sex, but when the broad-brimmed sombrero was pulled well down on her head, when the cartridge-belt and the six-gun were slung about her waist, and most of all when she spurred her mount recklessly across the hills no one could have suspected that this was not some graceful boy born and bred in the mountain-desert, willful as a young mountain lion, and as dangerous.

"Sleepy?" called Wilbur.

She waited a moment and then queried with exaggerated impudence: "Well?"

Ennui unspeakable was in that drawling monotone.

"Brace up; I've got news for you. And I've brought Pierre along to tell you about it."

"Oh!"

And she sat bolt upright with shining eyes. Instantly she remembered to yawn again, but her glance smiled on them above her hand.

She apologized. "Awfully sleepy, Dick."

But he was not deceived. He said: "There's a dance down near the Barnes place, and Pierre wants you to go with him."

"Pierre! A dance?"

He explained: "Dick's lost his head over a girl with yellow hair, and he wants me to go down and see her. He thought you might want to go along."

89

Her face changed like the moon when a cloud blows across it. She answered with another slow, insolent yawn: "Thanks! I'm staying home tonight."

Wilbur glared his rage covertly at Pierre, but the latter was blandly unconscious that he had made any *faux pas*.

He said carelessly: "Too bad. It might be interesting. Jack?"

At his voice she looked up—a sharp and graceful toss of her head.

"What?"

"The girl with the yellow hair."

"Then go ahead and see her. I won't keep you. You don't mind if I go on sleeping? Sit down and be at home."

With this she calmly turned her back again and seemed thoroughly disposed to carry out her word.

Red Pierre flushed a little, watching her, and he spoke his anger outright: "You're acting like a sulky kid, Jack, not like a man."

It was a habit of his to forget that she was a woman. Without turning her head she answered: "Do you want to know why?"

"You're like a cat showing your claws. Go on! Tell me what the reason is."

"Because I get tired of you."

In all his life he had never been so scorned. He did not see the covert grin of Wilbur in the background. He blurted: "Tired?"

"Awfully. You don't mind me being frank, do you, Pierre?"

He could only stammer: "Sometimes I wish to God you *were* a man, Jack!"

"You don't often remember that I'm a woman."

"Do you mean that I'm rude or rough with you, Jacqueline?"

Still the silence, but Wilbur was grinning broader than ever. "Answer me!"

She started up and faced him, her face convulsed with rage.

"What do you want me to say? Yes, you are rude—I hate you and your lot. Go away from me; I don't want you; I hate you all."

And she would have said more, but furious sobs swelled her throat and she could not speak, but dropped, face down, on the bunk and gripped the blankets in each hard-set hand. Over her Pierre leaned, utterly bewildered, found nothing that he could say, and then turned and strode, frowning, from the room. Wilbur hastened after him and caught him just as the door was closing.

"Come back," he pleaded. "This is the best game I've ever seen. Come back, Pierre! You've made a wonderful start."

Pierre le Rouge shook off the detaining hand and glared up at Wilbur.

"Don't try irony, Dick. I feel like murder. Think of it! All this time she's been hating me; and now it's making her weep; think of it—Jack—weeping!"

"Why, you're a child, Pierre. She's in love with you."

"With me?"

"With Red Pierre."

"You can't make a joke out of Jack with me. You ought to know that."

"Pierre, I'd as soon make a joke out of a wildcat."

"Grinning still? Wilbur, I'm taking more from you than I would from any man on the ranges."

"I know you are, and that's why I'm stringing this out because I'm going to have a laugh—ha, ha, ha!—the rest of my life—ha, ha, ha!—whenever I think of this!"

The burst of merriment left him speechless, and Pierre,

glowering, his right hand twitching dangerously close to that holster at his hip. He sobered, and said: "Go in and talk to her and prove that I'm right."

"Ask Jack if she loves me? Why, I'd as soon ask any man the same question."

The big long-rider was instantly curious.

"Has she never appealed to you as a woman, Pierre?"

"How could she? I've watched her ride; I've watched her use her gun; I've slept rolled in the same blankets with her, back to back; I've walked and talked and traveled with her as if she were my kid brother."

Wilbur nodded, as if the miracle were being slowly unfolded before his eyes.

"And you've never noticed anything different about her? Never watched a little lift and grace in her walk that no man could ever have; never seen her color change just because you, Pierre, came near or went far away from her?"

"Because of me?" asked the bewildered Pierre.

"You fool, you! Why, lad, I've been kept amused by you two for a whole evening, watching her play for your attention, saving her best smiles for you, keeping her best attitudes for you, and letting all the richness of her voice go out for—a block—a stone. Gad, the thing still doesn't seem possible! Pierre, one instant of that girl would give romance to a man's whole life."

"This girl? This Jack of ours?"

"He hasn't seen it! Why, if I hadn't seen years ago that she had tied her hands and turned her heart over to you, I'd have been begging her for a smile, a shadow of a hope."

"If I didn't know you, Dick, I'd say that you were partly drunk and partly a fool."

"Here's a hundred—a cold hundred that I'm right. I'll make it a thousand, if you dare."

"Dare what?"

"Ask her to marry you."

"Marry—me?"

"Damn it all—well, then—whatever you like. But I say that if you go back into that room and sit still and merely look at her, she'll be in your arms within five minutes."

"I hate to take charity, but a bet is a bet. That hundred is in my pocket already. It's a go!"

They shook hands.

"But what will be your proof, Dick, whether I win or lose?"

"Your face, blockhead, when you come out of the room."

Upon this Pierre pondered a moment, and then turned toward the door. He set his hand on the knob, faltered, and finally set his teeth and entered the room.

18

She lay as he had left her, except that her face was now pillowed in her arms, and the long sobs kept her body quivering. Curiosity swept over Pierre, looking down at her, but chiefly a puzzled grief such as a man feels when a friend is in trouble. He came closer and laid a hand on her shoulder.

"Jack!"

She turned far enough to strike his hand away and instantly resumed her former position, though the sobs were softer. This childish anger irritated him. He was about to storm out of the room when the thought of the hundred dollars stopped him. The bet had been made, and it seemed unsportsmanlike to leave without some effort.

The effort which he finally made was that suggested by Wilbur. He folded his arms and stood silent, waiting, and ready to judge the time as nearly as he could until the five minutes should have elapsed. He was so busy computing the minutes that it was with a start that he noticed some time later that the weeping had ceased. She lay quiet. Her hand was dabbing furtively at her face for a purpose which Pierre could not surmise.

At last a broken voice murmured: "Pierre!"

He would not speak, but something in the voice made his anger go. After a little it came, and louder this time: "Pierre?"

He did not stir.

She whirled and sat on the edge of the bunk, crying: "Pierre!" with a note of fright.

Still he persisted in that silence, his arms folded, the keen blue eyes considering her as if from a great distance.

She explained: "I was afraid—Pierre! Why don't you speak? Tell me, are you angry?"

And she sprang up and made a pace toward him. She had never seemed so little manlike, so wholly womanly. And the hand which stretched toward him, palm up, was a symbol of everything new and strange that he found in her.

He had seen it balled to a small, angry fist, brown and dangerous; he had seen it gripping the butt of a revolver, ready for the draw; he had seen it tugging at the reins and holding a racing horse in check with an ease which a man would envy; but never before had he seen it turned palm up, to his knowledge; and now, because he could not speak to her, according to his plan, he studied her thoroughly for the first time.

Slender and marvelously made was that hand. The

whole woman was in it, made for beauty, not for use. It was all he could do to keep from exclaiming.

She made a quick step toward him, eager, uncertain: "Pierre, I thought you had left me—that you were gone, and angry."

Something caught on fire in Pierre, but still he would say nothing. He was beginning to feel a cruel pleasure in his victory, but it was not without a deep sense of danger.

She had laid aside her six-gun, but she had not abandoned it. She had laid aside her anger, but she could resume it again as swiftly as she could take up her revolver.

She cried with a little burst of rage: "Pierre, you are making a game of me!"

But seeing that he did not change she altered swiftly and caught his hand in both of hers. She spoke the name which she always used when she was greatly moved.

"Ah, Pierre le Rouge, what have I done?"

His silence tempted her on like the smile of the sphinx.

And suddenly she was inside his arms, though how she separated them he could not tell, and crying: "Pierre, I am unhappy. Help me, Pierre!"

It was true, then, and Wilbur had won his bet. But how could it have happened? He took the arms that encircled his neck and brought them slowly down, and watched her curiously. Something was expected of him, but what it was he could not tell, for women were as strange to him as the wild sea is strange to the Arab.

He hunted his mind, and then: "One of the boys has angered you, Jack?"

And she said, because she could think of no way to cover the confusion which came to her after the outbreak: "Yes."

He dropped her arms and strode a pace or two up and down the room.

"Gandil?"

"N-no!"

"You're lying. It was Gandil."

And he made straight for the door.

She ran after him and flung herself between him and the door. Clearly, as if it were a painted picture, she saw him facing Gandil—saw their hands leap for the guns— saw Gandil pitch face forward on the floor. "Pierre—for God's sake!"

Her terror convinced him partially, and the furor went back from his eyes as a light goes back in a long, dark hall.

"On your honor, Jack, it's not Gandil?"

"On my honor."

"But someone has broken you up. And he's here—he's one of us, this man who's bothered you."

She could not help but answer: "Yes."

He scowled down at the floor.

"You would never be able to guess who it is. Give it up. After all—I can live through it—I guess."

He took her face between his hands and frowned down into her eyes. "Tell me his name, Jack, and the dog—"

She said: "Let me go. Take your hands away, Pierre."

He obeyed her, deeply worried, and she stood up for a moment with a hand pressed over her eyes, swaying. He had never seen her like this; he was like a pilot striving to steer his ship through an unfathomable fog. Following what had become an instinct with him, he raised his left hand and touched the cross beneath his throat. And inspiration came to him.

19

"Whether you want to or not, Jack, we'll go to this dance tonight."

Jacqueline's hand fell away from her eyes. She seemed suddenly glad again.

"Do you want to take me, Pierre?"

He explained: "Of course. Besides, we have to keep an eye on Wilbur. This girl with the yellow hair—"

She had altered swiftly again. There was no understanding her or following her moods this day. He decided to disregard them, as he had often done before.

"Black Gandil swears that I'm bringing bad luck to the boys at last. Patterson has disappeared; Wilbur has lost his head about a girl. We've got to save Dick."

He knew that she was fond of Wilbur, but she showed no enthusiasm now.

"Let him go his own way. He's big enough to take care of himself."

"But it's common talk, Jack, that the end of Wilbur will come through a woman. It was that that sent him on the long trail, you know. And this girl with the yellow hair—"

"Why do you harp on her?"

"Harp on her?"

"Every other word—nothing but yellow hair. I'm sick of it. I know the kind—faded corn color—dyed, probably. Pierre, you are all blind, and you most of all."

This being obviously childish, Pierre brushed the consideration of it from his mind.

97

"And for clothes, Jack?"

They were both dumb. It had been years since she had worn the clothes of a woman. She had danced with the men of her father's gang many a time while someone whistled or played on a mouth-organ, and there was the time they rode into Beulah Ferry and held up the dance hall, and Jim Boone and Mansie lined up the crowd with their hands held high above their heads while the sweating musicians played fast and furious and Jack and Pierre danced down the center of the hall.

She had danced many a time, but never in the clothes of a woman; so they stared, mutely puzzled.

A though came first to Jacqueline. She stepped close and murmured her suggestion in the ear of Pierre. Whatever it was, it made his jaw set hard and brought grave lines into his face.

She stepped back, asking: "Well?"

"We'll do it. What a little demon you are, Jack!"

"Then we'll have to start now. There's barely time."

They ran from the room together, and as they passed through the room below Wilbur called after them: "The dance?"

"Yes."

"Wait and go with me."

"We ride in a roundabout way."

They were through the door as Pierre called back, and a moment later the hoofs of their horses scattered the gravel down the hillside. Jacqueline rode a black stallion sired by her father's mighty Thunder, who had grown old but still could do the work of three ordinary horses in carrying the great bulk of his master. The son of Thunder was little like his sire, but a slender-limbed racer, graceful, nervous, eager. A clumsy rider would have ruined the horse in a single day's hard work among the trails of the mountain-desert, but Jacqueline, fairly reading the mind

98

of the black, nursed his strength when it was needed and let him run free and swift when the ground before him was level.

Now she picked her course dexterously down the hillside with the cream-colored mare of Pierre following half a length behind.

After the first down-pitch of ground was covered they passed into difficult terrain, and for half an hour went at a jog trot, winging in and out among the rocks, climbing steadily up and up through the hills.

Here the ground opened up again, and they roved on at a free gallop, the black always half a length in front. Along the ridge of a crest, an almost level stretch of a mile or more, Jack eased the grip on the reins, and the black responded with a sudden lengthening of stride and lowered his head with ears pressed back flat while he fairly flew over the ground.

Nothing could match that speed. The strong mare fell to the rear, fighting gamely, but beaten by that effort of the stallion.

Jack swerved in the saddle and looked back, laughing her triumph. Pierre smiled grimly in response and leaned forward, shifting his weight more over the withers of Mary. He spoke to her, and one of her pricking ears fell back as if to listen to his voice. He spoke again and the other ear fell back, her neck straightened, she gave her whole heart to her work.

First she held the stallion even, then she began to gain. That was the meaning of those round, strong hips, and the breadth of the chest. She needed a half-mile of running to warm her to her work, and now the black came back to her with every leap.

The thunder of the approaching hoofs warned the girl. One more glance she cast in apprehension over her shoulder, and then brought her spurs into play again and again.

Still the rush of hoofs behind her grew louder and louder, and now there was a panting at her side and the head of cream-colored Mary drew up and past.

She gave up the battle with a little shout of anger and slowed up her mount with a sharp pull on the reins. It needed only a word from Pierre and his mare drew down to a hand-gallop, twisting her head a little toward the black as if she called for some recognition of her superiority.

"It's always this way," cried Jack, and jerked at the reins with a childish impotence of anger. "I beat you for the first quarter of a mile and then this fool of a horse—I'm going to give him away."

"The black," said Pierre, assuming an air of quiet and superior knowing which always aggravated her most, "is a good second-rate cayuse when someone who knows horses is in the saddle. I'd give you fifty for him on the strength of his looks and keep him for a decoration."

She could only glare her speechless rage for a moment. Then she changed swiftly and threw out her hands in a little gesture of surrender.

"After all, what difference does it make? Your Mary can beat him in a long run or a short one, but it's your horse, Pierre, and that takes the sting away. If it were anyone else's I'd—well, I'd shoot either the horse or the rider. But my partner's horse is my horse, you know."

He swerved his mare sharply to the left and took her hand with a strong grip.

"Jack, of all the men I've ever known, I'd rather ride with you, I'd rather fight for you."

"Of all the *men* you ever knew," she said, "I suppose that I am."

He did not hear the low voice, for he was looking out over the canyon. A few moments later they swung out onto the very crest of the range.

On all sides the hills dropped away through the gloom

of the evening, brown nearby, but falling off through a faint blue haze and growing blue-black with the distance. A sharp wind, chill with the coming of night, cut at them. Not a hundred feet overhead shot a low-winging hawk back from his day's hunting and rising only high enough to clear the range and then plunge down toward his nest.

Like the hawks they peered down from their point of vantage into the profound gloom of the valley below. They shaded their eyes and studied it with a singular interest for long moments, patient, as the hawk.

So these two marauders stared until she raised a hand slowly and then pointed down. He followed the direction she indicated, and there, through the haze of the evening, he made out a glimmer of lights.

He said sharply: "I know the place, but we'll have a devil of a ride to get there."

And like the swooping hawk they started down the slope. It was precipitous in many places, but Pierre kept almost at a gallop, making the mare take the slopes often crouched back on her haunches with forefeet braced forward, and sliding many yards at a time.

In between the boulders he darted, twisting here and there, and always erect and jaunty in the saddle, swaying easily with every movement of the mare. Not far behind him came the girl. Fine rider that she was, she could not hope to compete with such matchless horsemanship where man and horse were only one piece of strong brawn and muscle, one daring spirit. Many a time the chances seemed too desperate to her, but she followed blindly where he led, setting her teeth at each succeeding venture, and coming out safe every time, until they swung out at last through a screen of brush and onto the level floor of the valley.

20

In the heart of that valley two roads crossed. Many a year before a man with some imagination and illimitable faith was moved by the crossing of those roads to build a general merchandise store.

Time justified his faith, in a small way, and now McGuire's store was famed for leagues and leagues about, for he dared to take chances with all manner of novelties, and the curious, when their pocketbooks were full, went to McGuire's to find inspiration.

Business was dull this night, however; there was not a single patron at the bar, and the store itself was empty, so he went to put out the big gasoline lamp which hung from the ceiling in the center of the room, and was on the ladder, reaching high above his head, when a singular chill caught him in the center of his plump back and radiated from that spot in all directions, freezing his blood. He swallowed the lump in his throat and with his arms still stretched toward the lamp he turned his head and glanced behind.

Two men stood watching him from a position just inside the door. How they had come there he could never guess, for the floor creaked at the lightest step. Nevertheless, these phantoms had appeared silently, and now they must be dealt with. He turned on the ladder to face them, and still he kept the arms automatically above his head while he descended to the floor.

However, on a closer examination, these two did not seem particularly formidable. They were both quite young, one with dark-red hair and a somewhat overbright eye; the other was hardly more than a boy, very slender, delicately made, the sort of handsome young scoundrel whom women cannot resist.

Having made these observations, McGuire ventured to lower his arms by jerks; nothing happened; he was safe. So he vented his feelings by scowling on the strangers.

"Well," he snapped, "what's up? Too late for business. I'm closin' up."

The two quite disregarded him. Their eyes were wandering calmly about the place, and now they rested on the pride of McGuire's store. The figure of a man in evening clothes, complete from shoes to gloves and silk hat, stood beside a girl of wax loveliness. She wore a low-cut gown of dark green, and over her shoulders was draped a scarf of dull gold. Above, a sign said: "You only get married once; why don't you do it up right?"

"That," said the taller stranger, "ought to do very nicely for us, eh?"

And the younger replied in a curiously light, pleasant voice: "Just what we want. But how'll I get away with all that fluffy stuff, eh?"

The elder explained: "We're going to a bit of a dance and we'll take those evening clothes."

The heart of McGuire beat faster and his little eyes took in the strangers again from head to foot.

"They ain't for sale," he said. "They's just samples. But right over here—"

"This isn't a question of selling," said the red-headed man. "We've come to accept a little donation, McGuire."

The storekeeper grew purple and white in patches. Still there was no show of violence, no display of guns; he moved his hand toward his own weapon, and still the strangers merely smiled quietly on him. He decided that he had misunderstood, and went on: "Over here I got a line of goods that you'll like. Just step up and—"

The younger man, frowning now, replied: "We don't want to see any more of your junk. The clothes on the models suit us all right. Slip 'em off, McGuire."

"But—" began McGuire and then stopped.

His first suspicion returned with redoubled force; above all, that head of dark red hair made him thoughtful. He finished hoarsely: "What the hell's this?"

"Why," smiled the taller man, "you've never done much in the interests of charity, and now's a good time for you to start. Hurry up, McGuire; we're late already!"

There was a snarl from the storekeeper, and he went for his gun, but something in the peculiarly steady eyes of the two made him stop with his fingers frozen hard around the butt.

He whispered: "You're Red Pierre?"

"The clothes," repeated Pierre sternly, "on the jump, McGuire."

And with a jump McGuire obeyed. His hands trembled so that he could hardly remove the scarf from the shoulders of the model, but afterward fear made his fingers supple, as he did up the clothes in two bundles.

Jacqueline took one of them and Pierre the other under his left arm; with his right hand he drew out some yellow coins.

"I didn't buy these clothes because I didn't have the time to dicker with you, McGuire. I've heard you talk prices before, you know. But here's what the clothes are worth to us."

And into the quaking hands of McGuire he poured a chinking stream of gold pieces.

Relief, amazement, and a very wholesome fear struggled in the face of McGuire as he saw himself threefold over-

paid. At that little yellow heap he remained staring, un-
heeding the sound of the retreating outlaws.

"It ain't possible," he said at last, "thieves have begun to
pay."

His eyes sought the ceiling.

"So that's Red Pierre?" said McGuire.

As for Pierre and Jacqueline, they were instantly safe in
the black heart of the mountains. Many a mile of hard
riding lay before them, however, and there was no road,
not even a trail that they could follow. They had never
even seen the Crittenden schoolhouse; they knew its loca-
tion only by vague descriptions.

But they had ridden a thousand times in places far more
bewildering and less known to them. Like all true denizens
of the mountain-desert, they had a sense of direction as
uncanny as that of an Eskimo. Now they struck off con-
fidently through the dark and trailed up and down
through the mountains until they reached a hollow in the
center of which shone a group of dim lights. It was the
schoolhouse near the Barnes place, the scene of the dance.

So they turned back behind the hills and in the covert of
a group of cottonwoods they kindled two more little fires,
shading them on three sides with rocks and leaving them
open for the sake of light on the fourth.

They worked busily for a time, without a word spoken
by either of them. The only sound was the rustling of
Jacqueline's stolen silks and the purling of a small stream
of water near them, some meager spring.

But presently: "P-P-Pierre, I'm f-freezing."

He himself was numbed by the chill air and paused in
the task of thrusting a leg into the trousers, which persisted in tangling and twisting under his foot.

"So'm I. It's c-c-cold as the d-d-d-devil."

"And these—th-things—aren't any thicker than spider
webs."

"Wait. I'll build you a great big fire."

And he scooped up a number of dead twigs.

There was an interlude of more silk rustling, then: "P-P-Pierre."

"Well?"

"I wish I had a m-m-m-mirror."

"Jack, are you vain?"

A cry of delight answered him. He threw caution to the winds and advanced on her. He found her kneeling above a pool of water fed by the soft sliding little stream from the spring. With one hand she held a burning branch by way of a torch, and with the other she patted her hair into shape and finally thrust the comb into the glittering, heavy coils.

She started, as if she felt his presence.

"P-P-Pierre!"

"Yes?"

"Look!"

She stood with the torch high overhead, and he saw a beauty so glorious that he closed his eyes involuntarily and still he saw the vision in the dull-green gown, with the scarf of old gold about her dazzling white shoulders. And there were two lights, the barbaric red of the jewels in her hair, and the black shimmer of her eyes. He drew back a step more. It was a picture to be looked at from a distance.

She ran to him with a cry of dismay: "Pierre, what's wrong with me?"

His arms went round her of their own accord. It was the only place they could go. And all this beauty was held in the circle of his will.

"It isn't that, but you're so wonderful, Jack, so glorious, that I hardly know you. You're like a different person."

He felt the warm body trembling, and the thought that it was not entirely from the cold set his heart beating like a trip-hammer. What he felt was so strange to him that he

106

stepped back in a vague alarm, and then laughed. She stood with an expectant smile.

"Jack, how am I to risk you in the arms of all the strangers in that dance?

"It's late. Listen!"

She cupped a hand at her ear and leaned to listen. Up from the hollow below them came a faint strain of music, a very light sound that was drowned a moment later by the solemn rushing of the wind through the great trees above them.

They looked up of one accord.

"Pierre, what was that?"

"Nothing; the wind in the branches, that's all."

"It was a hushing sound. It was like—it was like a warning, almost."

But he was already turning away, and she followed him hastily.

21

Jacqueline could never ride a horse in that gown, or even sit sidewise in the saddle without hopelessly crumpling it, so they walked to the schoolhouse. It was a slow progress, for she had to step lightly and carefully for fear of the slippers. He took her bare arm and helped her; he would never have thought of it under ordinary conditions, but since she had put on this gown she was greatly changed to him, no longer the wild, free rider of the mountain-desert, but a defenseless, strangely weak being. Her strength was now something other than the skill to ride hard and shoot straight and quick.

So they came to the schoolhouse and reached the long line of buggies, buckboards, and, most of all, saddled horses. They crowded the horse-shed where the school children stabled their mounts in the winter weather. They were tethered to the posts of the fence; they were grouped about the trees.

It was a prodigious gathering, and a great affair for the mountain-desert. They knew this even before they had set foot within the building.

They stopped here and adjusted their masks carefully. They were made from a strip of black lining which Jack had torn from one of the coats in the trunk which lay far back in the hills.

Those masks had to be tied firmly and well, for some jester might try to pull away that of Pierre, and if his face were seen, it would be death—a slaughter without defense, for he had not been able to conceal his big Colt in these tight-fitting clothes. Even as it was, there was peril from the moment that the lights within should shine on that head of dark-red hair.

As for Jack, there was little fear that she would be recognized. She was strange even to Pierre every time he looked down at her, for she had ceased to be Jack and had become very definitely "Jacqueline." But the masks were on; the scarf adjusted about the throat and bare, shivering shoulders of Jack, and they stood arm in arm before the door out of which streamed the voices and the music.

"Are you ready?"

"Yes."

But she was trembling so, either from fear, or excitement, or both, that he had to take a firm hold on her arm and almost carry her up the steps, shove the door open, and force her in.

A hundred eyes were instantly upon them, practiced, suspicious eyes, accustomed to search into all things and take nothing for granted; eyes of men who, when a rap came at the door, looked to see whether or not the shadow of the stranger fell full in the center of the crack beneath the door. If it fell to one side the man might be an enemy, and therefore they would stand at one side of the room, their hands upon the butt of a six-gun, and shout: "Come in." Such was the battery of glances from the men, and the color of Pierre altered, paled.

He knew some of those faces, for those who hunt and are hunted never forget the least gestures of their enemies. There was a mighty temptation to turn back even then, but he set his teeth and forced himself to stand calmly.

The chuckle which replied to this maneuver freed him for the moment. Suspicion was lulled. Moreover, the red-jeweled hair of Jacqueline and her lighted eyes called all attention almost immediately upon her. She shifted the golden scarf—the white arms and breast flashed in the light—a gasp responded. There would be talk tomorrow; there were whispers even now.

It was not the main hall that they stood in, for this school, having been built by an aspiring community, contained two rooms; this smaller room, used by the little ones of the school, was now converted into a hat-and-cloak room.

Pierre hung up his hat, removed his gloves slowly, nerving himself to endure the sharp glances, and opened the door for Jacqueline.

If she had held back tremulously before, something she had seen in the eyes of those in the first room, something in the whisper and murmur which rose the moment she started to leave, gave her courage. She stepped into the dance-hall like a queen going forth to address devoted subjects.

The second ordeal was easier than the first. There were many times more people in that crowded room, but each was intent upon his own pleasure. A wave of warmth and light swept upon them, and a blare of music, and a stir and hum of voices, and here and there the sweet sound of a happy girl's laughter. They raised their heads, these two wild rangers of the mountain-desert, and breathed deep of the fantastic scene.

There was no attempt at beauty in the costumes of the masqueraders. Here and there some girl achieved a novel and pleasing effect; but on the whole they strove for cheaper and more stirring things in the line of the grotesque.

Here passed a youth wearing a beard made from the stiff, red bristles of the tail of a sorrel horse. Another wore a bear's head cunningly stuffed, the grinning teeth flashing over his head and the skin draped over his shoulders. A third disfigured himself by painting after the fashion of an Indian on the warpath, with crimson streaks down his forehead and red and black across his cheeks.

But not more than a third of all the assembly made any effort to masquerade, beyond the use of the simple black mask across the upper part of the face. The rest of the men and women contented themselves with wearing the very finest clothes they could afford to buy, and there was through the air a scent of the general merchandise store which not even a liberal use of cheap perfume and all the drifts of pale-blue cigarette smoke could quite overcome.

As for the music, it was furnished by two very old men, relics of the days when there were contests in fiddling; a stout fellow of middle age, with cheeks swelled almost to bursting as he thundered out terrific blasts on a slide trombone; a youth who rattled two sticks on an overturned dish-pan in lieu of a drum, and a cornetist of real skill.

There were hard faces in the crowd, most of them, of

men who had set their teeth against hard weather and hard men, and fought their way through, not to happiness, but to existence, so that fighting had become their pleasure.

Now they relaxed their eternal vigilance, their eternal suspicion. Another phase of their nature weakened. Some of them were smiling and laughing for the first time in months, perhaps, of labor and loneliness on the range. With the gates of good-nature opened, a veritable flood of gaiety burst out. It glittered in their eyes, it rose to their lips in a wild laughter. They seemed to be dancing more furiously fast in order to forget the life which they had left, and to which they must return.

These were the conquerors of the bitter nature of the mountain-desert. There was beauty here, the beauty of strength in the men and a brown loveliness in the girls; just as in the music, the blatancy of the rattling dish-pan and the blaring trombone were more than balanced by the real skill of the violinists, who kept a high, sweet, singing tone through all the clamor.

And Pierre le Rouge and Jacqueline? They stood aghast for a moment when that crash of noise broke around them; but they came from a life where there was nothing of beauty except the lonely strength of the mountains and the appalling silences of the stars that roll above the desert. Almost at once they caught the overtone of human joyousness, and they turned with smiles to each other, and it was "Pierre?" "Jack?" Then a nod, and she was in his arms, and they glided into the dance.

22

When a crowd gathers in the street, there rises a babel of voices, a confused and pointless clamor, no matter what the purpose of the gathering, until some man who can think as well as shout begins to speak. Then the crowd murmurs a moment, and after a few seconds composes itself to listen.

So it was with the noise in the hall when Pierre and Jacqueline began to dance. First there were smiles of derision and envy around them, but after a moment a little hush came where they moved.

They could not help but dance well, for they had youth and grace and strength, and the glances of applause and envy were like wine to quicken their blood, while above all they caught the overtone of the singing violins, and danced by that alone. The music ended with a long flourish just as they whirled to a stop in a corner of the room. At once an eddy of men started toward them.

"Who shall it be?" smiled Pierre. "With whom do you want to dance? It's your triumph, Jack."

She was alight and alive with the victory, and her eyes roved over the crowd.

"The big man with the tawny hair."

"But he's making right past us."

"No; he'll turn and come back."

"How do you know?"

For answer she glanced up and laughed, and he realized with a singular sense of loneliness that she knew many things which were beyond his ken. Someone touched his arm, and a voice, many voices, beset him.

"How's the chances for a dance with the girl, partner?"

"This dance is already booked," Pierre answered, and kept his eyes on the tall man with the scarred face and the resolute jaw. He wondered why Jacqueline had chosen such a partner.

At least she had prophesied correctly, for the big man turned toward them just as he seemed about to head for another part of the hall. The crowd gave way before him, not that he shouldered them aside, but they seemed to feel the coming of his shadow before him, and separated as they would have done before the shadow of a falling tree.

In another moment Pierre found himself looking up to the giant. No mask could cover that long, twisting mark of white down his cheek, nor hide the square set of the jaw, nor dim the steady eyes.

And there came to Pierre an exceedingly great uneasiness in his right hand, and a twitching of the fingers low down on his thigh where the familiar holster should have hung. His left hand rose, following the old instinct, and touched beneath his throat where the cold cross lay.

He was saying easily: "This is your dance, isn't it?"

"Right, Bud," answered the big man in a mellow voice as great as his size. "Sorry I can't swap partners with you, but I hunt alone."

An overwhelming desire to get a distance between himself and this huge unknown came to Pierre.

He said: "There goes the music. You're off."

And the other, moving toward Jack, leaned down a little and murmured at the ear of the outlaw: "Thanks, Pierre."

Then he was gone, and Jacqueline was laughing over his shoulder back to Pierre.

Through his daze and through the rising clamor of the

113

music, a voice said beside him: "You look sort of sick, dude. Who's your friend?"

"Don't you know him?" asked Pierre.

"No more than I do you; but I've ridden the range for ten years around here, and I know that he's new to these parts. If I'd ever glimpsed him before, I'd remember him. He'd be a bad man in a mix, eh?"

And Pierre answered with devout earnestness: "He would."

"But where 'd you buy those duds, pal? Hey, look! Here's what I've been waiting for—the Barneses and the girl that's visitin' 'em from the East."

"What girl?"

"Look!"

The Barnes group was passing through the door, and last came the unmistakable form of Dick Wilbur, masked, but not masked enough to hide his familiar smile or cover the well-known sound of his laughter as it drifted to Pierre across the hall, and on his arm was a girl in an evening dress of blue, with a small, black mask across her eyes, and deep-golden hair.

Pausing before she swung into the dance with Wilbur, she made a gesture with the white arm, and looked up laughing to big, handsome Dick. Pierre trembled with a red rage when he saw the hands of Wilbur about her.

Dick, in passing, marked Pierre's stare above the heads of the crowd, and frowned with trouble. The hungry eyes of Pierre followed them as they circled the hall again; and this time Wilbur, perhaps fearing that something had gone wrong with Pierre, steered close to the edge of the dancing crowd and looked inquisitively across.

He leaned and spoke to the girl, and she turned her head, smiling, to Pierre. Then the smile went out, and even despite the mask, he saw her eyes widen. She stopped and slipped from the arm of Wilbur, and came step by step slowly toward him like one walking in her sleep.

There, by the edge of the dancers, with the noise of the music and the shuffling feet to cover them, they met. The hands she held to him were cold and trembling.

"Is it you?"

"It is I."

That was all; and then the shadow of Wilbur loomed above them.

"What's this? Do you know each other? It isn't possible! Pierre, are you playing a game with me?"

But under the glance of Pierre he fell back a step, and reached for the gun which was not there. They were alone once more.

"Mary—Mary Brown!"

"Pierre!"

"But you are dead!"

"No, no! But you—Pierre, where can we go?"

"Outside."

"Let us go quickly!"

"Do you need a wrap?"

"No."

"But it is cold outside, and your shoulders are bare."

"Then take that cloak. But quickly, Pierre, before we're followed."

He drew it about her; he led her through the door; it clicked shut; they were alone with the sweet, frosty air before them. She tore away the mask.

"And yours, Pierre?"

"Not here."

"Why?"

"Because there are people. Hurry. Now here, with just the trees around us—"

And he tore off his mask.

The white, cold moon shone over them, slipping down between the dark tops of the trees, and the wind stirred slowly through the branches with a faint, hushing sound, as if once more a warning were coming to Pierre this night.

He looked up, his left hand at the cross.

"Look down. You are afraid of something, Pierre. What is it?"

"With your arms around my neck, there's nothing in the world I fear. I never dreamed I could love anything more than the little girl who lay in the snow, and died there that night."

"And I never dreamed I could smile at any man except the boy who lay by me that night. And he died."

"What miracle saved you?"

She said: "It was wonderful, and yet very simple. You remember how the tree crushed me down into the snow? Well, when the landslide moved, it carried the tree before it; the weight of the trunk was lifted from me. Perhaps it was a rock that struck me over the head then, for I lost consciousness. The slide didn't bury me, but the rush carried me before it like a stick before a wave, you see.

"When I woke I was almost completely covered with a blanket of debris, but I could move my arms, and managed to prop myself up in a sitting posture. It was there that my father and his searching party found me; he had been combing that district all night. They carried me back, terribly bruised, but without even a bone broken. It was a miracle that I escaped, and the miracle must have been worked by your cross; do you remember?"

He shuddered. "The cross—for every good fortune it has brought me, it has brought bad luck to others. I'll throw it away, now—and then—no, it makes no difference. We are done for."

"Pierre!"

"Don't you see, Mary, or are you still blind as I was ever since I saw you tonight? It's all in that name—Pierre."

"There's nothing in it, Pierre, that I don't love."

His head was bowed as if with the weight of the words which he foresaw.

"You have heard of the wild men of the mountains, and the long-riders?"

He knew that she nodded, though she could not speak.

"I am Red Pierre."

"You!"

"Yes."

Yet he had the courage to raise his head and watch her shrink with horror. It was only an instant. Then she was beside him again, and one arm around him, while she turned her head and glanced fearfully back at the lighted schoolhouse. The faint music mocked them.

"And you dared to come to the dance? We must go. Look, there are horses! We'll ride off into the mountains, and they'll never find us—we'll—"

"Hush! One day's riding would kill you—riding as I ride."

"I'm strong—very strong, and the love of you, Pierre, will give me more strength. But quickly, for if they knew you, every man in that place would come armed and ready to kill. I know, for I've heard them talk. Tell me, are one-half of all the terrible things they say—"

"They are true, I guess."

"I won't think of them. Whatever you've done, it was not you, but some devil that forced you on. Pierre, I love you more than ever. Will you go East with me, and home? We will lose ourselves in New York. The millions of the crowd will hide us."

"Mary, there are some men from whom even the night can't hide me. If they were blind their hate would give them eyes to find me."

"Pierre, you are not turning away from me—Pierre— There's some ghost of a chance for us. Will you take that chance and come with me?"

He thought of many things, but what he answered was: "I will."

117

"Then let's go at once. The railroad—"

"Not that way. No one in that house suspects me now. We'll go back and put on our masks again, and—hush. What's there?"

"Nothing."

"There is—a man's step."

And she, seeing the look on his face, covered her eyes in horror. When she looked up a great form was looming through the dark, and then the voice of Wilbur came, hard and cold.

"I've looked everywhere for you. Miss Brown, they are anxious about you in the schoolhouse. Will you go back?"

"No—I—"

But Pierre commanded: "Go back."

So she turned, and he ordered again: "I think our friend has something to say to me. You can find your way easily. Tomorrow—"

"Tomorrow, Pierre?"

"Yes."

"I shall be waiting."

With what a voice she said it! And then she was gone. He turned quietly to big Dick Wilbur, on whose contorted face the moonlight fell.

"Say it, Dick, and have it out in cursing me, if that'll help."

The big man stood with his hands gripped behind, fighting for self-control.

"Pierre, I've cared for you more than I've cared for any other man. I've thought of you like a kid brother. Now tell me that you haven't done this thing, and I'll believe you rather than my senses. Tell me you haven't stolen the girl I love away from me; tell me—"

"I love her, Dick."

"Damn you! And she?"

"She'll forget me; God knows I hope she'll forget me."

"I brought two guns with me. Here they are."

He held out the weapons.

"Take your choice."

"Does it have to be this way?"

"If you'd rather have me shoot you down in cold blood?"

"I suppose this is as good a way as any."

"What do you mean?"

"Nothing. Give me a gun."

"Here. This is ten paces. Are you ready?"

"Yes."

"Pierre. God forgive you for what you've done. She liked me, I know. If it weren't for you, I would have won her and a chance for real life again—but now—damn you!"

"I'll count to ten, slowly and evenly. When I reach ten we fire?"

"Yes."

"I'll trust you not to beat the count, Dick."

"And I you. Start."

He counted quietly, evenly: "One, two, three, four, five, six, seven, eight, nine—ten!"

The gun jerked up in the hand of Wilbur, but he stayed the movement with his finger pressing still upon the trigger. The hand of Pierre had not moved.

He cried: "By God, Pierre, what do you mean?"

There was no answer. He strode across the intervening space, dropped his gun and caught the other by the shoulders. Out of Pierre's nerveless fingers the revolver slipped to the ground.

"In the name of God, Pierre, what has happened to you?"

"Dick, why didn't you fire?"

"Fire? Murder you?"

"You shoot straight—I know—it would have been over quickly."

"What is it, boy? You look dead—there's no color in your

face, no light in your eyes, even your voice is dead. I know it isn't fear. What is it?"

"You're wrong. It's fear."

"Fear and Red Pierre. The two don't mate."

"Fear of living, Dick."

"So that's it? God help you. Pierre, forgive me. I should have known that you had met her before, but I was mad, and didn't know what I was doing, couldn't think."

"It's over and forgotten. I have to go back and get Jack. Will you ride home with us?"

"Jack? She's not in the hall. She left shortly after you went, and she means some deviltry. There's a jealous fiend in that girl. I watched her eyes when they followed you and Mary from the hall."

"Then we'll ride back alone."

"Not I. Carry the word to Jim that I'm through with the game. I'm going to wash some of the grime off my conscience and try to make myself fit to speak to this girl again."

"It's the cross," said Pierre.

"What do you mean?"

"Nothing. The bad luck has come to poor old Jim at last, because he saved me out of the snow. Patterson has gone, and now you, and perhaps Jack—well, this is good-bye, Dick?"

"Yes."

Their hands met.

"You forgive me, Dick?"

"With all my heart, old fellow."

"I'll try to wish you luck. Stay close to her. Perhaps you'll win her."

"I'll do what one man can."

"But if you succeed, ride out of the mountain-desert with her—never let me hear of it."

"I don't understand. Will you tell me what's between

you, Pierre? You've some sort of claim on her. What is it?"

"I've said good-bye. Only one thing more. Never mention my name to her."

So he turned and walked out into the moonlight and Wilbur stared after him until he disappeared beyond the shoulder of a hill.

23

It was early morning before Pierre reached the refuge of Boone's gang, but there was still a light through the window of the large room, and he entered to find Boone, Mansie, and Gandil grouped about the fire, all ominously silent, all ominously wakeful. They looked up to him and big Jim nodded his gray head. Otherwise there was no greeting.

From a shadowy corner Jacqueline rose and went toward the door. He crossed quickly and barred the way.

"What is it, Jack?"

"Get out of the way."

"Not till you tell me what's wrong."

A veritable devil of fury came blazing in her eyes, and her hand twitched nervously back to her hip where the dark holster hung. She said in a voice that shook with anger: "Don't try your bluff on me. I ain't no shorthorn, Pierre le Rouge."

He stepped aside, frowning.

"Tomorrow I'll argue the point with you, Jack."

She turned at the door and snapped back: "You? You ain't fast enough on the draw to argue with me!"

And she was gone. He turned to face the mocking smile of Black Gandil and a rapid volley of questions.

"Where's Patterson?"

"No more idea than you have."

"And Branch?"

"What's become of Branch? Hasn't he returned?"

"No. And Dick Wilbur?"

"Boys, he's done with this life and I'm glad of it. He's starting on a new track."

"After a woman?" sneered Bud Mansie.

"Shut up, Bud," broke in Boone, and then slowly to Pierre: "Patterson is gone for two days now. You ought to know what that means. Branch ought to have returned from looking for him, and Branch is still out. Wilbur is gone. Out of seven we're only four left. Who's next?"

He stared gloomily from face to face, and Gandil snarled: "A fellow who saves a shipwrecked man—"

"Damn you, keep still, Gandil."

"Don't damn me, Pierre le Rouge, but damn the luck you've brought to Jim Boone."

"Jim, do you chalk all this up against me?"

"I, lad? No, no! But it's queer. Patterson's done for; there's no doubt of that. Good-natured Garry Patterson. God, boy, how we'll miss him! And Branch seems to have gone the same way. If neither of them show up before morning we can cross 'em off the list. Now Wilbur has gone and Jack has ridden home looking like a small-sized thunderstorm, and now you come with a white face and a blank eye. What hell is trailin' us, Pierre, what hell is in store for us. You've seen something, and we want to know what it is."

"A ghost, Jim, that's all."

Bud Mansie said softly: "There's only one ghost that could make you look like this. Was it McGurk, Pierre?"

Boone commanded: "No more of that, Bud. Boys, we're going to turn in, and tomorrow we'll climb the hills looking for the two we've lost. But there's something or someone after us. Lads, I'm thinking our good days are over. The seven of us have been too many for a small posse and too fast for a big one, but the seven are down to four. The good days are over."

And the three answered in a solemn chorus: "The good days are over."

All eyes fixed on Pierre, and his glance was settled on the floor.

The morning brought them no better cheer, for Jack, whose singing generally wakened them, was not to be coaxed into speech, and when Pierre entered the room she rose and left the breakfast table. The sad eyes of Jim Boone followed her and then turned to Pierre. No explanation was forthcoming, and he asked for none. The old fatalist had accepted the worst, and now he waited for doom to descend.

They took their horses after breakfast and rode out to search the hills, for it was quite possible that an accident had crippled at least one of the two lost men, either Patterson or Branch. Not a gully within miles was left unsearched, but toward evening they rode back, one by one, with no tidings.

One by one they rode up, and whistled to announce their coming, and then rode on to the stable to unsaddle their horses. About the supper table all gathered with the exception of Bud Mansie. So they waited the meal and each from time to time stole a glance at the fifth plate where Bud should sit.

It was Jack who finally stirred herself from her dumb gloom to take up that fifth and carry it out of the room. It was as if she had announced the death of Mansie.

After that, they ate what they could and then went back around the fire. The evening waned, but it brought no sign of any of the missing three. The wood burned low in the fire. The first to break the long silence was Jim Boone, with "Who brings in the wood?"

And Black Gandil answered: "We'll match, eh?"

In an outburst of energy the day before he disappeared Garry Patterson had chopped up some wood and left a pile of it at the corner of the house. It was a very little thing to bring in an armful of that wood, but long-riders do not love work, and now they started the matching seriously. The odd man was out, and Pierre went out on the first toss of the coins.

"You see," said Gandil. "Bad luck to everyone but himself."

At the next throw Jacqueline was the lucky one, and her father afterward. Gandil rose and stretched himself leisurely, yet as he sauntered toward the door his backward glance at Pierre was black indeed. He glanced curiously toward Jack—who looked away sharply—and then turned his eyes to her father.

The latter was considering him with a gloomy, foreboding stare and considering over and over again, as Pierre le Rouge well knew, the prophecy of Black Morgan Gandil.

He fell in turn into a solemn brooding, and many a picture out of the past came up beside him and stood near till he could almost feel its presence. He was roused by the creaking of the floor beneath the ponderous step of Jim Boone, who flung the door open and shouted: "Oh, Morgan."

In the silence he turned and stared back at Pierre.

"What's up with Gandil?"

"God knows, not I."

Pierre rose and ran from the room and around the side of the building. There by the woodpile lay the prostrate body. It was a mere limp weight when he turned and raised it in his arms. So he walked back into the house carrying all that was left of Black Morgan Gandil, and placed his burden on a bunk at the side of the room.

There had been no outcry from either Jim Boone or his daughter, but they came quickly to him, and Jacqueline pressed her ear over the heart of the hurt man.

She said: "He's still alive, but nearly gone. Where's the wound?"

They found it when they drew off his coat—a small cut high on the right breast, and another lower and more to the left. Either of them would have been fatal, and about each the flesh was discolored where the hilt of the knife or the fist of the striker had driven home the blade.

They stood back and made no hopeless effort to save him. It was uncanny that Black Morgan Gandil, after all of his battles, should die without a struggle in this way. And it had been no cowardly attack from the rear. Both wounds were in the front. A hope came to them when his color increased at one time, but it was for only a moment; it went out again as if someone were erasing paint from his cheeks.

But just as they were about to turn away his body stirred with a slight convulsion, the eyes opened wide, and he strove to speak. A red froth came on his lips. He made another desperate effort, and twisting himself onto one elbow pointed a rigid arm at Pierre. He gasped: "McGurk—God!" and dropped. He was dead before his head touched the blanket.

It was Jacqueline who closed the staring eyes, for the two men were frozen where they stood. They had heard the story of Patterson and Branch and Mansie in one word from the lips of the dying man.

McGurk was back. McGurk was prowling about the last of the gang of Boone, and the lone wolf had pulled down four of the band one by one on successive days. Only two remained, and these two looked at one another with a common thought.

"The lights!" cried Jacqueline, turning from the body of

125

Gandil. "He can shoot us down through the windows at his leisure."

"But he won't," said her father. "I've lived too long with the name of McGurk in my ears not to know the man. He'll never kill by stealth, but openly and man to man. I know him, damn him. He'll wait till he meets us alone, and then we'll finish as poor Gandil, there, or Patterson and Branch and Bud Mansie, all of them fallen somewhere in the mountains with the buzzards left to bury 'em. That's how we'll finish with McGurk on our trail. And you—Gandil was right—it's you that's brought him on us. A ship-wrecked man—by God, Gandil was right!"

His right hand froze on the butt of his gun and his face convulsed with impotent rage, for he knew, as both the others knew, that long before that gun was clear of the holster the bullet from Pierre's gun would be on its way. But Pierre threw his arms wide, and standing so, his shadow made a black cross on the wall behind him. He even smiled to tempt the big man further.

24

Jacqueline ran between and caught the hand of her father, crying:

"Are you going to finish the work of McGurk before he has a chance to start it? He hunted the rest down one by one. Dad, if you put out Pierre what is left? Can you face that devil alone?"

And the old man groaned: "But it's his luck that's ruined me. It's his damned luck which has broken up the finest fellowship that ever mocked at law on the ranges. Oh, Jack, the heart in me's broken. I wish to God that I lay where Gandil lies. What's the use of fighting any longer? No man can stand up against McGurk!"

And the cold which had come in the blood of Pierre agreed with him. He was a slayer of men, but McGurk was a devil incarnate. His father had died at the hand of this lone rider; it was fitting, it was fate that he himself should die in the same way. The girl looked from face to face, and sensed their despondency. It seemed that their fear gave her the greater courage. Her face flushed as she stood glaring her scorn.

"The yellow streak took a long time in showin', but it's in you, all right, Pierre le Rouge."

"You've hated me ever since the dance, Jack. Why?"

"Because I knew you were yellow—like this!"

He shrugged his shoulders like one who gives up the fight against a woman, and seeing it, she changed suddenly and made a gesture with both hands toward him, a sudden gesture filled with grace and a queer tenderness.

She said: "Pierre, have you forgotten that when you were only a boy you stood up to McGurk and drew blood from him? Are you afraid of him now?"

"I'll take my chance with any man—but McGurk—"

"He has no cross to bring him luck."

"Aye, and he has no friends for that luck to ruin. Look at Gandil, Jack, and then speak to me of the cross."

"Pierre, that first time you met you almost beat him to the draw. Oh, if I were a man, I'd—Pierre, it was to get McGurk that you rode out to the range. You've been here six years, and McGurk is still alive, and now you're ready to run from his shadow."

"Run?" he said hotly. "I swear to God that as I stand here

I've no fear of death and no hope for the life ahead."

She sneered: "You're white while you say it. Your will may be brave, but your blood's a coward, Pierre. It deserts you."

"Jack, you devil—"

"Aye, you can threaten me safely. But if McGurk were here—"

"Let him come."

"Then give me one promise."

"A thousand of 'em."

"Let me hunt him with you."

He stared at her with wonder.

"Jack, what a heart you have! If you were a man we could rule the mountains, you and I."

"Even as I am, what prevents us, Pierre?"

And looking at her he forgot the sorrow which had been his ever since he looked up to the face framed with red-gold hair and the dark tree behind and the cold stars steady above it. It would come to him again, but now it was gone, and he murmured, smiling: "I wonder?"

They made their plans that night, sitting all three to-gether. It was better to go out and hunt the hunter than to wait there and be tracked down. Jack, for she insisted on it, would ride out with Pierre the next morning and hunt through the hills for the hiding-place of McGurk.

Some covert he must have, so as to be near his victims. Nothing else could explain the ease with which he kept on their track. They would take the trail, and Jim Boone, no longer agile enough to be effective on the trail, would guard the house and the body of Gandil in it.

There was little danger that even McGurk would try to rush a hostile house, but they took no chances. The guns of Jim Boone were given a thorough overhauling, and he wore as usual at his belt the heavy-handled hunting knife, a deadly weapon in a hand-to-hand fight. Thus equipped, they left him and took the trail.

They had not ridden a hundred yards when a whistle followed them, the familiar whistle of the gang. They reined short and saw big Dick Wilbur riding his bay after them, but at some distance he halted and shouted: "Pierre!"

"He's come back to us!" cried Jack.

"No. It's only some message."

"Do you know?"

"Yes. Stay here. This is for me alone."

And he rode back to Wilbur, who swung his horse close alongside. However hard he had followed in the pursuit of happiness, his face was drawn with lines of age and his eyes circled with shadows.

He said: "I've kept close on her trail, Pierre, and the nearest she has come to kindness has been to send me back with a message to you."

He laughed without mirth, and the sound stopped abruptly.

"This is the message in her own words: 'I love him, Dick, and there's nothing in the world for me without him. Bring him back to me. I don't care how; but bring him back.' So tell Jack to ride the trail alone today and go back with me. I give her up, not freely, but because I know there's no hope for me."

But Pierre answered: "Wherever I've gone there's been luck for me and hell for everyone around me. I lived with a priest, Dick, and left him when I was nearly old enough to begin repaying his care. I came South and found a father and lost him the same day. I gambled for money with which to bury him, and a man died that night and another was hurt. I escaped from the town by riding a horse to death. I was nearly killed in a landslide, and now the men who saved me from that are done for.

"It's all one story, the same over and over. Can I carry a fortune like that back to her? Dick, it would haunt me by day and by night. She would be the next. I know it as I

129

know that I'm sitting in the saddle here. That's my answer. Carry it back to her."

"I won't lie and tell you I'm sorry, because I'm a fool and still have a ghost of a hope, but this will be hard news to tell her, and I'd rather give five years of life than face the look that will come in her eyes."

"I know it, Dick."

"But this is final?"

"It is."

"Then good-bye again, and—God bless you, Pierre."

"And you, old fellow."

They swerved their horses in opposite directions and galloped apart.

"It was nothing," said Pierre to Jack, when he came up with her and drew his horse down to a trot. But he knew that she had read his mind.

But all day through the mazes of canyon and hill and rolling ground they searched patiently. There was no cranny in the rocks too small for them to reconnoiter with caution. There was no group of trees they did not examine.

Yet it was not strange that they failed. In the space of every square mile there were a hundred hiding-places which might have served McGurk. It would have taken a month to comb the country. They had only a day, and left the result to chance, but chance failed them. When the shadows commenced to swing across the gullies they turned back and rode with downward heads, silent.

One hill lay between them and the old ranch house which had been the headquarters for their gang so many days, when they saw a faint drift of smoke across the sky— not a thin column of smoke such as rises from a chimney, but a broad stream of pale mist, as if a dozen chimneys were spouting wood smoke at once.

They exchanged glances and spurred their horses up

the last slope. As always in a short spurt, the long-legged black of Jacqueline out-distanced the cream-colored mare, and it was she who first topped the rise of land. The girl whirled in her saddle with raised arm, screamed back at Pierre, and rode on at a still more furious pace.

What he saw when he reached a corresponding position was the ranch house wreathed in smoke, and through all the lower windows was the red dance of flames. Before him fled Jacqueline with all the speed of the black. He loosened the reins, spoke to the mare, and she responded with a mighty rush. Even that tearing pace could not quite take him up to the girl, but he flung himself from the saddle and was at her side when she ran across the smoking veranda and wrenched at the front door.

The whole frame gave back at her, and as Pierre snatched her to one side the doorway fell crashing on the porch, while a mighty volume of smoke burst out at them like a puff from the pit.

They stood sputtering, coughing, and choking, and when they could look again they saw a solid wall of red flame, thick, impenetrable, shuddering with the breath of the wind.

While they stared a stronger breath of that wind tore the wall of flames apart, driving it back in a raging tide to either side. The fire had circled the walls of the entire room, but it had scarcely encroached on the center, and there, seated at the table, was Boone.

He had scarcely changed from the position in which they last saw him, save that he was fallen somewhat deeper in the chair, his head resting against the top of the back. He greeted them, through that infernal furnace, with laughter, and wide, steady eyes. At least it seemed laughter, for the mouth was agape and the lips grinned back, but there was no sound from the lips and no light in the fixed eyes.

Laughter indeed it was, but it was the laughter of death, as if the soul of the man, in dying, recognized its natural wild element and had burst into convulsive mirth. So he sat there, untouched as yet by the wide river of fire, chuckling at his destiny. The wall of fire closed across the doorway again and the work of red ruin went on with a crashing of timbers from the upper part of the building.

As that living wall shut solidly, Jacqueline leaped forward, shouting, like a man, words of hope and rescue; Pierre caught her barely in time—a precarious grasp on the wrist from which she nearly wrenched herself free and gained the entrance to the fire. But the jerk threw her off balance for the least fraction of an instant, and the next moment she was safe in his arms.

Safe? He might as well have held a wildcat, or captured with his bare hands a wild eagle, strong of talon and beak. She tore and raged in a wild fury.

"Pierre, coward, devil!"

"Steady, Jack!"

"Are you going to let him die?"

"Don't you see? He's already dead."

"You lie. You only fear the fire!"

"I tell you, McGurk has been here before us."

Her arm was freed by a twisting effort and she beat him furiously across the face. One blow cut his lip and a steady trickle of hot blood left a taste of salt in his mouth.

"You young fiend!" he cried, and grasped both her wrists with a crushing force.

She leaned and gnashed at his hands, but he whirled her about and held her from behind, impotent, raging still.

"A hundred McGurks could never have killed him!"

There was a sharp explosion from the midst of the fire.

"See! He's fighting against his death!"

"No! No! It's only the falling of a timber!"

Yet with a panic at his heart he knew that it was the sharp crack of a firearm.

"Liar again! Pierre, for God's sake, do something for him. Father! He's fighting for his life!"

Another and another explosion from the midst of the fire. He understood then.

"The flames have reached his guns. That's all, Jack. Don't you see? We'd be throwing ourselves away to run into those flames."

Realization came to her at last. A heavy weight slumped down suddenly over his arms. He held her easily, lightly. Her head had tilted back, and the red flare of the fire beat across her face and throat. The roar of the flames shut out all other thought of the world and cast a wide inferno of light around them.

Higher and higher rose the fires, and the wind cut off great fragments and hurried them off into the night, blowing them, it seemed, straight up against the piled thunder of the clouds. Then the roof sagged, swayed, and fell crashing, while a vast cloud of sparks and livid fires shot up a hundred feet into the air. It was as if the soul of old Boone had departed in that final flare.

It started the girl into sudden life, surprising Pierre, so that she managed to wrench herself free and ran from him. He sprang after her with a shout, fearing that in her hysteria she might fling herself into the fire, but that was not her purpose. Straight to the black horse she ran, swung into the saddle with the ease of a man, and rode furiously off through the falling of the night.

He watched her with a curious closing of loneliness like a hand about his heart. He had failed, and because of that failure even Jacqueline was leaving him. It was strange, for since the loss of the girl of the yellow hair and those deep blue eyes, he had never dreamed that another thing in life could pain him.

So at length he mounted the mare again and rode slowly down the hill and out toward the distant ranges, trotting mile after mile with downward head, not caring even if

McGurk should cross him, for surely this was the final end of the world to Pierre le Rouge.

About midnight he halted at last, for the uneasy sway of the mare showed that she was nearly dead on her feet with weariness. He found a convenient place for a camp, built his fire, and wrapped his blanket about him without thinking of food.

He never knew how long he sat there, for his thoughts circled the world and back again and found all a prospect of desert before him and behind, until a sound, a vague sound out of the night, startled him into alertness. He slipped from beside the fire and into the shadow of a steep rock, watching with eyes that almost pierced the dark on all sides.

And there he saw her creeping up on the outskirts of the firelight, prone on her hands and knees, dragging herself up like a young wildcat hunting prey; it was the glimmer of her eyes that he caught first through the gloom. A cold thought came to him that she had returned with her gun ready.

Inch by inch she came closer, and now he was aware of her restless glances probing on all sides of the camp-fire. Silence—only the crackling of a pitchy stick. And then he heard a muffled sound, soft, soft as the beating of a heart in the night, and regularly pulsing. It hurt him infinitely, and he called gently: "Jack, why are you weeping?"

She started up with her fingers twisted at the butt of her gun.

"It's a lie," called a tremulous voice. "Why should I weep?"

And then she ran to him.

"Oh, Pierre, I thought you were gone!"

That silence which came between them was thick with understanding greater than speech. He said at last: "I've made my plan. I am going straight for the higher moun-

134

tains and try to shake McGurk off my trail. There's one chance in ten I may succeed, and if I do then I'll wait for my chance and come down on him, for sooner or later we have to fight this out to the end."

"I know a place he could never find," said Jacqueline. "The old cabin in the gulley between the Twin Bears. We'll start for it tonight."

"Not we," he answered. "Jack, here's the end of our riding together."

She frowned with puzzled wonder.

He explained: "One man is stronger than a dozen. That's the strength of McGurk—that he rides alone. He's finished your father's men. There's only Wilbur left, and Wilbur will go next—then me!"

She stretched her hands to him. She seemed to be pleading for her very life.

"But if he finds us and has to fight us both—I shoot as straight as a man, Pierre!"

"Straighter than most. And you're a better pal than any I've ever ridden with. But I must go alone. It's only a lone wolf that will ever bring down McGurk. Think how he's rounded us up like a herd of cattle and brought us down one by one."

"By getting each man alone and killing him from behind."

"From the front, Jack. No, he's fought square with each one. The wounds of Black Gandil were all in front, and when McGurk and I meet it's going to be face to face."

Her tone changed, softened: "But what of me, Pierre?"

"You have to leave this life. Go down to the city, Jack. Live like a woman; marry some lucky fellow; be happy."

"Can you leave me so easily?"

"No, it's hard, devilish hard to part with a pal like you, Jack; but all the rest of my life I've got hard things to face, partner."

"Partner!" she repeated with an indescribable emphasis. "Pierre, I can't leave you."

"Why?"

"I'm afraid to go. Let me stay!"

He said gloomily: "No good will come of it."

"I'll never trouble you—never!"

"No, the bad luck comes on the people who are with me, but never on me. It's struck them all down, one by one; your turn is next, Jack. If I could leave the cross behind—"

He covered his face and groaned: "But I don't dare; I don't dare! I have to face McGurk. Jack, I hate myself for it, but I can't help it. I'm afraid of McGurk, afraid of that damned white face, that lowered, fluttering eyelid, that sneering mouth. Without the cross to bring me luck, how could I meet him? But while I keep the cross there's ruin and hell without end for everyone with me."

She was white and shaking. She said: "I'm not afraid. I've one friend left; there's nothing else to care for."

"So it's to be this way, Jack?"

"This way, and no other."

"Partner, I'm glad. My God, Jack, what a man you would have made!"

Their hands met and clung together, and her head had drooped, perhaps in acquiescence.

25

Dick Wilbur, telling Mary how Pierre had cut himself adrift, did not even pretend to sorrow, and she listened to him with her eyes fixed steadily on his own. As a matter of fact, she had shown neither hope nor excitement from the moment he came back to her and started to tell his message. But if she showed neither hope nor excitement for herself, surely she gave Dick still fewer grounds for any optimistic foresights.

So he finished gloomily: "And as far as I can make out, Pierre is right. There's some rotten bad luck that follows him. It may not be the cross—I don't suppose you believe in superstition like that, Miss Brown?"

She said: "It saved my life."

"The cross?"

"Yes."

"Then Pierre—you mean—you met before the dance—you mean—"

He was stammering so that he couldn't finish his thoughts, and she broke in: "If he will not come to me, then I must go to him."

"Follow Pierre le Rouge?" queried Wilbur. "You're an optimist. But that's because you've never seen him ride. I consider it a good day's work to start out with him and keep within sight till night, but as for following and overtaking him—"

He laughed heartily at the thought.

And she smiled a little sadly, answering: "But I have the most boundless patience in the world. He may gallop all the way, but I will walk, and keep on walking, and reach him in the end."

Her hands moved out as though testing their power, gripping at the air.

"Where will you go to hunt for him?"

"I don't know. But every evening, when I look out at the sunset hills, with the purple along the valleys, I think that he must be out there somewhere, going toward the highest ranges. If I were up in that country I know that I could find him."

"Never in a thousand years."

"Why?"

"Because he's on the trail—"

"On the trail?"

"Of McGurk."

She started.

"What is this man McGurk? I hear of him on all sides. If one of the men rides a bucking horse successfully, some- one is sure to say: 'Who taught you what you know, Bud— McGurk?' And then the rest laugh. The other day a man was pointed out to me as an expert shot. 'Not as fast as McGurk,' it was said, 'but he shoots just as straight.' Finally I asked someone about McGurk. The only answer I re- ceived was: 'I hope you never find out what he is.' Tell me, what is McGurk?"

Wilbur considered the question gravely.

He said at last: "McGurk is—hell!"

He expanded his statement: "Think of a man who can ride anything that walks on four feet, who never misses with either a rifle or a revolver, who doesn't know the meaning of fear, and then imagine that man living by himself and fighting the rest of the world like a lone wolf. That's McGurk. He's never had a companion; he's never trusted any man. Perhaps that's why they say about him the same thing that they say about me."

"What's that?"

"You will smile when you hear. They say that McGurk will lose out in the end on account of some woman."

"And they say that of you?"

"They say right of me. I know it myself. Look at me now. What right have I here? If I'm found I'm the meat of the first man who sights me, but here I stay, and wait and watch for your smiles—like a love-sick boy. By God, you must despise me, Mary!"

"I don't try to understand you Westerners," she an- swered, "and that's why I have never questioned you before. Tell me, why is it that you come so stealthily to see me and run away as soon as anyone else appears?"

He said with wonder: "Haven't you guessed?"

"I don't dare guess."

"But you have, and your guess was right. There's a price on my head. By right, I should be out there on the ranges with Pierre le Rouge and McGurk. There's the only safe place; but I saw you and I came down out of the wilds and can't go back. I'll stay, I suppose, till I run my head into a halter."

She was too much moved to speak for a moment, and then: "You come to me in spite of that? Dick, whatever you have done, I know that it's only chance which made you go wrong, just as it made Pierre. I wish—"

The dimness of her eyes encouraged him with a hope. He moved closer to her.

He repeated: "You wish—"

"That you could be satisfied with a mere friendship. I could give you that, Dick, with all my heart."

He stepped back and smiled somewhat grimly on her.

She went on: "And this McGurk—what do you mean when you say that Pierre is on his trail?"

"Hunting him with a gun."

She grew paler, but her voice remained steady.

"But in all those miles of mountains they may never meet?"

"They can't stay apart any more than iron can stay away from a magnet. Listen: half a dozen years ago McGurk had the reputation of bearing a charmed life. He had been in a hundred fights and he was never touched with either a knife or a bullet. Then he crossed Pierre le Rouge when Pierre was only a youngster just come onto the range. He put two bullets through Pierre, but the boy shot him from the floor and wounded him for the first time. The charm of McGurk was broken.

"For half a dozen years McGurk was gone; there was

139

never a whisper about him. Then he came back and went on the trail of Pierre. He has killed the friends of Pierre one by one; Pierre himself is the next in order—Pierre or myself. And when those two meet there will be the greatest fight that was ever staged in the mountain-desert."

She stood straight, staring past Wilbur with hungry eyes.

"I knew he needed me. I have to save him, Dick. You see that? I have to bring him down from the mountains and keep him safe from McGurk. McGurk! Somehow the sound means what 'devil' used to mean to me."

"You've never traveled alone, and yet you'd go up there and brave everything that comes for the sake of Pierre? What has he done to deserve it, Mary?"

"What have I done, Dick, to deserve the care you have for me?"

He stared gloomily on her.

"When do you start?"

"Tonight."

"Your friends won't let you go."

"I'll steal away and leave a note behind me."

"And you'll go alone?"

She caught at a hope.

"Unless you'll go with me, Dick?"

"I? Take you—to Pierre?"

She did not speak to urge him, but in the silence her beauty pleaded for her.

He said: "Mary, how lovely you are. If I go I will have you for a few days—for a week at most, all to myself."

She shook her head. From the window behind her the sunset light flared in her hair, flooding it with red-gold.

"All the time that we are gone, you will never say things like this, Dick?"

"I suppose not. I should be near you, but terribly far away from your thoughts all the while. Still, you will be near. You will be very beautiful, Mary, riding up the trail

140

through the pines, with all the scents of the evergreens blowing about you, and I—well, I must go back to a second childhood and play a game of suppose—"

"A game of what?"

"Of supposing that you are really mine, Mary, and riding out into the wilderness for my sake."

She stepped a little closer, peering into his face.

"No matter what you suppose, I'm sure you'll leave that part of it merely a game, Dick!"

He laughed suddenly, though the sound broke off as short and sharp as it began.

"Haven't I played a game all my life with the fair ladies? And have I anything to show for it except laughter? I'll go with you, Mary, if you'll let me."

"Dick, you've a heart of gold! What shall I take?"

"I'll make the pack up, and I'll be back here an hour after dark and whistle. Like this—"

And he gave the call of Boone's gang.

"I understand. I'll be ready. Hurry, Dick, for we've very little time."

He hesitated, then: "All the time we're on the trail you must be far from me, and at the end of it will be Pierre le Rouge—and happiness for you. Before we start, Mary, I'd like to—"

It seemed that she read his mind, for she slipped suddenly inside his arms, kissed him, and was gone from the room. He stood a moment with a hand raised to his face.

"After all," he muttered, "that's enough to die for, and—" He threw up his long arms in a gesture of resignation.

"The will of God be done!" said Wilbur, and laughed again.

26

She was ready, crouched close to the window of her room, when the signal came, but first she was not sure, because the sound was as faint as a memory. Moreover, it might have been a freakish whistling in the wind, which rose stronger and stronger. It had piled the thunder-clouds higher and higher, and now and again a heavy drop of rain tapped at her window like a thrown pebble.

So she waited, and at last heard the whistle a second time, unmistakably clear. In a moment she was hurrying down to the stable, climbed into the saddle, and rode at a cautious trot out among the sand-hills.

For a time she saw no one, and commenced to fear that the whole thing had been a gruesomely real, practical jest. So she stopped her horse and imitated the signal whistle as well as she could. It was repeated immediately behind her—almost in her ear, and she turned to make out the dark form of a tall horseman.

"A bad night for the start," called Wilbur. "Do you want to wait till tomorrow?"

She could not answer for a moment, the wind whipping against her face, while a big drop stung her lips.

She said at length: "Would a night like this stop Pierre— or McGurk?"

For answer she heard his laughter.

"Then I'll start. I must never stop for weather."

He rode up beside her.

"This is the start of the finish."

"What do you mean?"

"Nothing. But somewhere on this ride, I've an idea a question will be answered for me."

"What question?"

Instead of replying he said: "You've got a slicker on?"

"Yes."

"Then follow me. We'll gallop into the wind a while and get the horses warmed up. Afterward we'll take the valley of the Old Crow and follow it up to the crest of the range."

His horse lunged out ahead of hers, and she followed, leaning far forward against a wind that kept her almost breathless. For several minutes they cantered steadily, and before the end of the gallop she was sitting straight up, her heart beating fast, a faint smile on her lips, and the blood running hot in her veins. For the battle was begun, she knew, by that first sharp gallop, and here at the start she felt confident of her strength. When she met Pierre she could force him to turn back with her.

Wilbur checked his horse to a trot; they climbed a hill, and just as the rain broke on them with a rattling gust they swung into the valley of the Old Crow. Above them in the sky the thunder rode; the rain whipped against the rocks like the rattle of a thousand flying hoofs; and now and again the lightning flashed across the sky.

Through that vast accompaniment they moved on in the night straight toward the heart of the mountains which sprang into sight with every flash of the lightning and seemed toppling almost above them, yet they were weary miles away, as she knew.

By those same flashes she caught glimpses of the face of Wilbur. She hardly knew him. She had seen him always big, gentle, handsome, good-natured; now he was grown harder, with a stern set of the jaw, and a certain square outline of face. It had seemed impossible. Now she began to guess how the law could have placed a price upon his head. For he belonged out here with the night and the crash of the storm, with strong, lawless things about him.

An awe grew in her, and she was filled half with dread and half with curiosity at the thought of facing him, as she must many a time, across the camp-fire. In a way, he was the ladder by which she climbed to an understanding of Pierre le Rouge, Red Pierre. For that Pierre, she knew, was to big Wilbur what Dick himself was to the great mass of law-abiding men. Accident had cut Wilbur adrift, but it was more than accident which started Pierre on the road to outlawry; it was the sheer love of dangerous chance, the glory in fighting other men. This was Pierre.

What was the man for whom Pierre hunted? What was McGurk? Not even the description of Wilbur had proved very enlightening. Her thought of him was vague, nebulous, and taking many forms. Sometimes he was tall and dark and stern. Again he was short and heavy and somewhat deformed of body. But always he was everywhere in the night about her.

All this she pondered as they began the ride up the valley, but as the long journey continued, and the hours and the miles rolled past them, a racking weariness possessed her and numbed her mind. She began to wish desperately for morning, but even morning might not bring an end to the ride. That would be at the will of the outlaw beside her. Finally, only one picture remained to her. It stabbed across the darkness of her mind—the red hair and the keen eyes of Pierre.

The storm decreased as they went up the valley. Finally the wind fell off to a pleasant breeze, and the clouds of the rain broke in the center of the heavens and toppled west in great tumbling masses. In half an hour's time the sky was clear, and a cold moon looked down on the blue-black evergreens, shining faintly with the wet, and on the dead black of the mountains.

For the first time in all that ride her companion spoke: "In an hour the gray will begin in the east. Suppose we camp here, eat, get a bit of sleep, and then start again?"

As if she had waited for permission, fighting against her weariness, she now let down the bars of her will, and a tingling stupor swept over her body and broke in hot, numbing waves on her brain.

"Whatever you say. I'm afraid I couldn't ride much further tonight."

"Look up at me."

She raised her head.

"No; you're all in. But you've made a game ride. I never dreamed there was so much iron in you. We'll make our fire just inside the trees and carry water up from the river, eh?"

A scanty growth of the evergreens walked over the hills and skirted along the valley, leaving a broad, sandy waste in the center where the river at times swelled with melted snow or sudden rains and rushed over the lower valley in a broad, muddy flood.

At the edge of the forest he picketed the horses in a little open space carpeted with wet, dead grass. It took him some time to find dry wood. So he wrapped her in blankets and left her sitting on a saddle. As the chill left her body she began to grow delightfully drowsy, and vaguely she heard the crack of his hatchet. He had found a rotten stump and was tearing off the wet outer bark to get at the dry wood within.

After that it was only a moment before a fire sputtered feebly and smoked at her feet. She watched it, only half conscious, in her utter weariness, and seeing dimly the hollow-eyed face of the man who stopped above the blaze. Now it grew quickly, and increased to a sharp-pointed pyramid of red flame. The bright sparks showered up, crackling and snapping, and when she followed their flight she saw the darkly nodding tops of the evergreens above her.

With the fire well under way, he took the coffeepot to get water from the river, and left her to fry the bacon. The fumes of the frying meat wakened her at once, and brushed even the thought of her exhaustion from her mind. She was hungry—ravenously hungry.

So she tended the bacon slices with care until they grew brown and crisped and curled at the edges. After that she removed the pan from the fire, and it was not until then that she began to wonder why Wilbur was so long in returning with the water. The bacon grew cold; she heated it again and was mightily tempted to taste one piece of it, but restrained herself to wait for Dick.

Still he did not come. She stood up and called, her high voice rising sharp and small through the trees. It seemed that some sound answered, so she smiled and sat down. Ten minutes passed and he was still gone. A cold alarm swept over her at that. She dropped the pan and ran out from the trees.

Everywhere was the bright moonlight—over the wet rocks, and sand, and glimmering on the slow tide of the river, but nowhere could she see Wilbur, or a form that looked like a man. Then the moonlight glinted on something at the edge of the river. She ran to it and found the coffee-can half in the water and partially filled with sand.

A wild temptation to scream came over her, but the tight muscles of her throat let out no sound. But if Wilbur were not here, where had he gone? He could not have vanished into thin air. The ripple of the water washing on the sand replied. Yes, that current might have rolled his body away.

To shut out the grim sight of the river she turned. Stretched across the ground at her feet she saw clearly the impression of a body in the moist sand.

27

The heels had left two deeply defined gouges in the ground; there was a sharp hollow where the head had lain, and a broad depression for the shoulders. It was the impression of the body of a man—a large man like Wilbur. Any hope, any doubt she might have had, slipped from her mind, and despair rolled into it with an even, sullen current, like the motion of the river.

It is strange what we do with our big moments of fear and sorrow and even of joy. Now Mary stooped and carefully washed out the coffee-pot, and filled it again with water higher up the bank; and turned back toward the edge of the trees.

It was all subconscious, this completing of the task which Wilbur had begun, and subconscious still was her careful rebuilding of the fire till it flamed high, as though she were setting a signal to recall the wanderer. But the flame, throwing warmth and red light across her eyes, recalled her sharply to reality, and she looked up and saw the dull dawn brightening beyond the dark evergreens.

Guilt, too, swept over her, for she remembered what big, handsome Dick Wilbur had said: He would meet his end through a woman. Now it had come to him, and through her.

She cringed at the thought, for what was she that a man should die in her service? She raised her hands with a moan to the nodding tops of the trees, to the vast, black sky above them, and the full knowledge of Wilbur's strength came to her, for had he not ridden calmly, defiantly, into the heart of this wilderness, confident in his power to care both for himself and for her? But she! What could she do wandering by herself? The image of Pierre le Rouge grew dim indeed and sad and distant.

She looked about her at the pack, which had been distributed expertly, and disposed on the ground by Wilbur. She could not even lash it in place behind the saddle. So she drew the blanket once more around her shoulders and sat down to think.

She might return to the house—doubtless she could find her way back. And leave Pierre in the heart of the mountains, surely lost to her forever. She made a determination, sullen, like a child, to ride on and on into the wilderness, and let fate take care of her. The pack she could bundle together as best she might; she would live as she might; and for a guide there would be the hunger for Pierre.

So she ended her thoughts with a hope; her head nodded lower, and she slept the deep sleep of the exhausted mind and body. She woke hours later with a start, instantly alert, quivering with fear and life and energy, for she felt like one who has gone to sleep with voices in his ear.

While she slept someone had been near her; she could have sworn it before her startled eyes glanced around.

And though she kept whispering, with white lips, "No, no; it is impossible!" yet there was evidence which proved it. The fire should have burned out, but instead it flamed more brightly than ever, and there was a little heap of fuel laid conveniently close. Moreover, both horses were saddled, and the pack lashed on the saddle of her own mount.

Whatever man or demon had done this work evidently intended that she should ride Wilbur's beautiful bay. Yes, for when she went closer, drawn by her wonder, she found that the stirrups had been much shortened.

Nothing was forgotten by this invisible caretaker; he had

even left out the cooking-tins, and she found a little batter of flapjack flour mixed.

The riddle was too great for solving. Perhaps Wilbur had disappeared merely to play a practical jest on her; but that supposition was too childish to be retained an instant. Perhaps—perhaps Pierre himself had discovered her, but having vowed never to see her again, he cared for her like the invisible hands in the old Greek fable.

This, again, an instinctive knowledge made her dismiss. If he were so close, loving her, he could not stay away; she read in her own heart, and knew. Then it must be something else; evil, because it feared to be seen; not wholly evil, because it surrounded her with care.

At least this new emotion obscured somewhat the terror and the sorrow of Wilbur's disappearance. She cooked her breakfast as if obeying the order of the unseen, climbed into the saddle of Wilbur's horse, and started off up the valley, leading her own mount.

Every moment or so she turned in the saddle suddenly in the hope of getting a glimpse of the follower, but even when she surveyed the entire stretch of country from the crest of a low hill, she saw nothing—not the least sign of life.

She rode slowly, this day, for she was stiff and sore from the violent journey of the night before, but though she went slowly, she kept steadily at the trail. It was a broad and pleasant one, being the beaten sand of the river-bottom; and the horse she rode was the finest that ever pranced beneath her.

His trot was as smooth and springy as the gallop of most horses, and when she let him run over a few level stretches, it was as if she had suddenly been taken up from the earth on wings. There was something about the animal, too, which reminded her of its vanished owner; for it had strength and pride and gentleness at once. Unquestionably it took kindly to its new rider; for once when she dismounted the big horse walked up behind and nuzzled her shoulder.

The mountains were much plainer before the end of the day. They rose sheer up in wave upon frozen wave like water piled ragged by some terrific gale, with the tops of the waters torn and tossed and then frozen forever in that position, like a fantastic and gargantuan mask of dreaming terror. It overawed the heart of Mary Brown to look up to them, but there was growing in her a new impulse of friendly understanding with all this scalped, bald region of rocks, as if in entering the valley she had passed through the gate which closes out the gentler world, and now she was admitted as a denizen of the mountain-desert, that scarred and ugly asylum for crime and fear and grandeur.

Feeling this new emotion, the old horizons of her mind gave way and widened; her gentle nature, which had known nothing but smiles, admitted the meaning of a frown. Did she not ride under the very shadow of that frown with her two horses? Was she not armed? She touched the holster at her hip, and smiled. To be sure, she could never hit a mark with that ponderous weapon, but at least the pistol gave the feeling of a dangerous lone rider, familiar with the wilds.

It was about dark, and she was on the verge of looking about for a suitable camping-place, when the bay halted sharply, tossed up his head, and whinnied. From the far distance she thought she heard the beginning of a whinny in reply. She could not be sure, but the possibility made her pulse quicken. In this region, she knew, no stranger could be a friend.

So she started the bay at a gallop and put a couple of swift miles between her and the point at which she had heard the sound; no living creature, she was sure, could have followed the pace the bay held during that distance. So, secure in her loneliness, she trotted the horse around a bend of the rocks and came on the sudden light of a camp-fire.

It was too late to wheel and gallop away; so she remained with her hand fumbling at the butt of the revolver, and her eyes fixed on the flicker of the fire. Not a voice accosted her. As far as she could peer among the lithe trunks of the saplings, not a sign of a living thing was near.

Yet whoever built that fire must be near, for it was obviously newly laid. Perhaps some fleeing outlaw had pitched his camp here and had been startled by her coming. In that case he lurked somewhere in the woods at that moment, his keen eyes fixed on her, and his gun gripped hard in his hand. Perhaps—and the thought thrilled her— this little camp had been prepared by the same power, human or unearthly, which had watched over her early that morning.

All reason and sane caution warned her to ride on and leave that camp unmolested, but an overwhelming, tingling curiosity besieged her. The thin column of smoke rose past the dark trees like a ghost, and reaching the unsheltered space above the trees, was smitten by a light wind and jerked away at a sharp angle.

She looked closer and saw a bed made of a great heap of the tips of limbs of spruce, a bed softer than down and more fragrant than any manufactured perfume, however costly.

Possibly it was the sight of this bed which tempted her down from the saddle, at last. With the reins over her arm, she stood close to the fire and warmed her hands, peering all the while on every side, like some wild and beautiful creature tempted by the bait of the trap, but shrinking from the scent of man.

As she stood there a broad, yellow moon edged its way above the hills and rolled up through the black trees and then floated through the sky. Beneath such a moon no harm could come to her. It was while she stared at it, letting her tensed alertness relax little by little, that she saw, or thought she saw, a hint of moving white pass over the top of the rise of ground and disappear among the trees.

She could not be sure, but her first impulse was to gather the reins with a jerk and place her foot in the stirrup; but then she looked back and saw the fire, burning low now and asking like a human voice to be replenished from the heap of small, broken fuel nearby; and she saw also the softly piled bed of evergreens.

She removed her foot from the stirrup. What mattered that imaginary figure of moving white? She felt a strong power of protection lying all about her, breathing out to her with the keen scent of the pines, fanning her face with the chill of the night breeze. She was alone, but she was secure in the wilderness.

28

For many a minute she waited by that camp-fire, but there was never a sign of the builder of it, though she centered all her will in making her eyes and ears sharper to pierce through the darkness and to gather from the thousand obscure whispers of the forest any sounds of human origin. So she grew bold at length to take off the pack and the saddles; the camp was hers, built for her coming by the invisible power which surrounded her, which read her mind, it seemed, and chose beforehand the certain route which she must follow.

She resigned herself to that force without question, and the worry of her search disappeared. It seemed certain that this omnipotence, whatever it might be, was reading her wishes and acting with all its power to fulfill them, so that in the end it was merely a question of time before she should accomplish her mission—before she should meet Pierre le Rouge face to face.

That night her sleep was deep, indeed, and she only wakened when the slant light of the sun struck across her eyes. It was a bright day, crisp and chill, and through the clear air the mountains seemed leaning directly above her, and chief of all two peaks, almost exactly similar, black monsters which ruled the range. Toward the gorge between them the valley of the Old Crow aimed its course, and straight up that diminishing canyon she rode all day.

The broad, sandy bottom changed and contracted until the channel was scarcely wide enough for the meager stream of water, and beside it she picked her way along a narrow path with banks on either side, which became with every mile more like cliffs, walling her in and dooming her to a single destination.

It was evening before she came to the headwaters of the Old Crow, and rode out into the gorge between the two mountains. The trail failed her here. There was no semblance of a ravine to follow, except the mighty gorge between the two peaks, and she ventured into the dark throat of this pass, riding through a gate with the guarding towers tall and black on either side.

The moment she was well started in it and the steep shadow of the evening fell across her almost like night from the west, her heart grew cold as the air. A sense of coming danger filled her. Yet she kept on, holding a tight rein, throwing many a fearful glance at the vast rocks which might have concealed an entire army in every mile of their extent.

When she found the cabin she mistook it at first for merely another rock of singular shape. It was at this shape that she stared, and checked her horse, and not till then did she note the faint flicker of a light no brighter than the phosphorescent glow of the eyes of a hunted beast.

Her impulse was to drive her spurs home and pass that place at a racing gallop, but she checked the impulse sharply and began to reason. In the first place, it was doubtless only the cabin of some prospector, such as she had often heard of. In the second place, night was almost upon her, and she saw no desirable camping-place, or at least any with the necessary water at hand.

What harm could come to her? Among Western men, she well knew a woman is safer than all the law and the police of the settled East can make her, so she nerved her courage and advanced toward the faint, changing light.

The cabin was hidden very cunningly. Crouched among the mighty boulders which earthquakes and storms of some wilder, earlier epoch had torn away from the side of the crags above, the house was like another stone, leaning its back to the mountain for support.

When she drew very close she knew that the light which glimmered at the window must come from an open fire, and the thought of a fire warmed her. She hallooed, and receiving no answer, fastened the horses and entered the house. The door swung to behind her, as if of its own volition it wished to make her a prisoner.

The place consisted of one room, and not a spacious one at that, but arranged as a shelter, not a home. The cooking, apparently, was done over the open hearth, for there was no sign of any stove, and, moreover, on the wall near the fireplace hung several soot-blackened pans and the inevitable coffeepot.

There were two bunks built on opposite sides of the room, and in the middle a table was made of a long section split from the heart of a log by wedges, apparently, and still rude and undressed, except for the preliminary smoothing off which had been done with a broad-ax.

The great plank was supported at either end by a roughly constructed sawbuck. It was very low, and for this reason two fairly square boulders of comfortable proportions were sufficiently high to serve as chairs.

For the rest, the furniture was almost too meager to suggest human habitation, but from nails on the wall there hung a few shirts and a pair of chaps, as well as a much-battered quirt. But a bucket of water in a corner suggested cleanliness, and a small, round, highly polished steel plate, hanging on the wall in lieu of a mirror, further fortified her decision that the owner of this place must be a man somewhat particular as to his appearance.

Here she interrupted her observations to build up the fire, which was flickering down and apparently on the verge of going out. She worked busily for a few minutes, and a roaring blaze rewarded her; she took off her slicker to enjoy the warmth, and in doing so, turned, and saw the owner of the place standing with folded arms just inside the door.

"Making yourself to home?" asked the host, in a low, strangely pleasant voice.

"Do you mind?" asked Mary Brown. "I couldn't find a place that would do for camping."

And she summoned her most winning smile. It was wasted, she knew at once, for the stranger hardened perceptibly, and his lip curled slightly in scorn or anger. In all her life Mary had never met a man so obdurate, and, moreover, she felt that he could not be wooed into a good humor.

"If you'd gone farther up the gorge," said the other,

"you'd of found the best sort of a campin' place—water and everything."

"Then I'll go," said Mary, shrinking at the thought of the strange, cold outdoors compared with this cheery fire. But she put on the slicker and started for the door.

At the last moment the host was touched with compunction. He called: "Wait a minute. There ain't no call to hurry. If you can get along here just stick around."

For a moment Mary hesitated, knowing that only the unwritten law of Western hospitality compelled that speech; it was the crackle and flare of the bright fire which overcame her pride.

She laid off the slicker again, saying, with another smile: "For just a few minutes, if you don't mind."

"Sure," said the other gracelessly, and tossed his own slicker onto a bunk.

Covertly, but very earnestly, Mary was studying him. He was hardly more than a boy—handsome, slender.

Now that handsome face was under a cloud of gloom, a frown on the forehead and a sneer on the lips, but it was something more than the expression which repelled Mary. For she felt that no matter how she wooed him, she could never win the sympathy of this darkly handsome, cruel youth; he was aloof from her, and the distance between them could never be crossed. She knew at once that the mysterious bridges which link men with women broke down in this case, and she was strongly tempted to leave the cabin to the sole possession of her surly host.

It was the warmth of the fire which once more decided against her reason, so she laid hands on one of the blocks of stone to roll it nearer to the hearth. She could not budge it. Then she caught the sneering laughter of the man, and strove again in a fury. It was no use; for the stone merely rocked a little and settled back in its place with a bump.

"Here," said the boy, "I'll move it for you."

It was a hard lift for him, but he set his teeth, raised the stone in his slender hands, and set it down again at a comfortable distance from the fire.

"Thank you," smiled Mary, but the boy stood panting against the wall, and for answer merely bestowed on her a rather malicious glance of triumph, as though he gloried in his superior strength and despised her weakness.

Some conversation was absolutely necessary, for the silence began to weigh on her. She said: "My name is Mary Brown."

"Is it?" said the boy, quite without interest. "You can call me Jack."

He sat down on the other stone, his dark face swept by the shadows of the flames, and rolled a cigarette, not deftly, but like one who is learning the mastery of the art. It surprised Mary, watching his fumbling fingers. She decided that Jack must be even younger than he looked.

She noticed also that the boy cast, from time to time, a sharp, rather worried glance of expectation toward the door, as if he feared it would open and disclose some important arrival. Furthermore, those old worn shirts hanging on the wall were much too large for the throat and shoulders of Jack.

Apparently, he lived there with some companion, and a companion of such a nature that he did not wish him to be seen by visitors. This explained the lad's coldness in receiving a guest; it also stimulated Mary to linger about a few more minutes.

29

Not that she stayed there without a growing fear, but she still felt about her, like the protection of some invisible cloak, the presence of the strange guide who had followed her up the valley of the Old Crow.

It seemed as if the boy were reading her mind.

"See you got two horses. Come up alone?"

"Most of the way," said Mary, and tingled with a rather feline pleasure to see that her curtness merely sharpened the interest of Jack.

The boy puffed on his cigarette, not with long, slow breaths of inhalation like a practiced smoker, but with a puckered face as though he feared that the fumes might drift into his eyes.

"Why," thought Mary, "he's only a child!"

Her heart warmed a little as she adopted this view of her surly host. Being warmed, and having much to say, words came of themselves. Surely it would do no harm to tell the story to this queer urchin, who might be able to throw some light on the nature of the invisible protector.

"I started with a man for guide." She fixed a searching gaze on the boy. "His name was Dick Wilbur."

She could not tell whether it was a tremble of the boy's hand or a short motion to knock off the cigarette ash.

"Did you say 'was' Dick Wilbur?"

"Yes. Did you know him?"

"Heard of him, I think. Kind of a hard one, wasn't he?"

"No, no! A fine, brave, gentle fellow—poor Dick!"

She stopped, her eyes filling with tears at many a memory.

"Hm!" coughed the boy. "I thought he was one of old Boone's gang? If he's dead, that made the last of 'em—except Red Pierre."

It was like the sound of a trumpet call at her ear. Mary sat up with a start.

"What do you know of Red Pierre?"

The boy flushed a little, and could not quite meet her eye.

"Nothin'."

"At least you know that he's still alive?"

"Sure. Anyone does. When he dies the whole range will know about it—damn quick. I know *that* much about Red Pierre; but who doesn't?"

"I, for one."

"You!"

Strangely enough, there was more of accusation than of surprise in the word.

"Certainly," repeated Mary. "I've only been in this part of the country for a short time. I really know almost nothing about the—the legends."

"Legends?" said the boy, and laughed. "Legend? Say, lady, if Red Pierre is just a legend the Civil War ain't no more'n a fable. Legend? You go anywhere on the range an' get 'em talking about that legend, and they'll make you think it's an honest-to-goodness fact, and no mistake."

Mary queried earnestly: "Tell me about Red Pierre. It's almost as hard to learn anything of him as it is to find out anything about McGurk."

"What you doing?" asked the boy, keen with suspicion. "Making a study of them two for a book?"

He wiped a damp forehead.

"Take it from me, lady, it ain't healthy to join up them two even in talk!"

"Is there any harm in words?"

The boy was so upset for some unknown reason that he rose and paced up and down the room.

"Lots of harm in fool words."

He sat down again, and seemed a little anxious to explain his unusual conduct.

"Ma'am, suppose you had a well plumb full of nitroglycerin in your back yard; suppose there was a forest fire comin' your way from all sides; would you like to have people talk about nitroglycerin and that forest fire meeting? Even the talk would give you chills. That's the way it is with Pierre and McGurk. When they meet there's going to be a fight that'll stop the hearts of the people that have to look on."

Mary smiled to cover her excitement.

"But are they coming your way?"

The question seemed to infuriate young Jack, who cried: "Ain't that a fool way of talkin'? Lady, they're coming everyone's way. You never know where they'll start from or where they'll land. If there's a thunder-cloud all over the sky, do you know where the lightning's going to strike?"

"Excuse me," said Mary, but she was still eager with curiosity, "but I should think that a youngster like you wouldn't have anything to fear from even those desperadoes."

"Youngster, eh?" snarled the boy, whose wrath seemed implacable. "I can make my draw and start my gun as fast as any man—except them two, maybe"—he lowered his voice somewhat even to name them—"Pierre—McGurk!"

"It seems hopeless to find out anything about McGurk," said Mary, "but at least you can tell me safely about Red Pierre."

"Interested in him, eh?" said the boy dryly.

"Well, he's a rather romantic figure, don't you think?"

"Romantic? Lady, about a month ago I was talking with a lady that was a widow because of Red Pierre. She didn't think him none too romantic."

"Red Pierre had killed the woman's husband?" repeated Mary, with pale lips.

"Yep. He was one of the gang that took a chance with Pierre and got bumped off. Had three bullets in him and dropped without getting his gun out of the leather. Pierre sure does a nice, artistic job. He serves you a murder with all the trimmings. If I wanted to die nice and polite without making a mess, I don't know who I'd rather go to than Red Pierre."

"A murderer!" whispered Mary, with bowed head.

The boy opened his lips to speak, but changed his mind and sat regarding the girl with a somewhat sinister smile.

"But might it not be," said Mary, "that he killed one man in self-defense and then his destiny drove him, and bad luck forced him into one bad position after another? There have been histories as strange as that, you know."

Jack laughed again, but most of the music was gone from the sound, and it was simply a low, ominous purr.

"Sure," he said. "You can take a bear-cub and keep him tame till he gets the taste of blood, but after that you got to keep him muzzled, you know. Pierre needs a muzzle, but there ain't enough gunfighters on the range to put one on him."

Something like pride crept into the boy's voice while he spoke, and he ended with a ringing tone. Then, feeling the curious, judicial eyes of Mary upon him, he abruptly changed the subject.

"You say Dick Wilbur is dead?"

"I don't know. I think he is."

"But he started out with you. You ought to know."

"It was like this: We had camped on the edge of the trees coming up the Old Crow Valley, and Dick went off with the can to get water at the river. He was gone a long time, and when I went out to look for him I found the can at the margin of the river half filled with sand, and beside it there was the impression of the body of a big man. That was all I found, and Dick never came back."

They were both silent for a moment.

"Could he have fallen into the river?"

"Sure. He was probably helped in. Did you look for the footprints?"

"I didn't think of that."

Jack was speechless with scorn.

"Sat down and cried, eh?"

"I was dazed; I couldn't think. But he couldn't have been killed by some other man. There was no shot fired; I should have heard it."

Jack moistened his lips.

"Lady, a knife don't make much sound either going or coming out—not much more sound than a whisper, but that whisper means a lot. I got an idea that Dick heard it. Then the river covered him up."

He stopped short and stared at Mary with squinted eyes.

"D'you mean to tell me that you had the nerve to come all the way up the Old Crow by yourself?"

"Every inch of the way."

Jack leaned forward, sneering, savage.

"Then I suppose you put the hitch that's on that pack outside?"

"No."

Jack was dumbfounded.

"Then you admit—"

"That first night when I went to sleep I felt as if there were something near me. When I woke up there was a bright fire burning in front of me and the pack had been lashed and placed on one of the horses. At first I thought that it was Dick, who had come back. But Dick didn't appear all day. The next night—"

"Wait!" said Jack. "This is gettin' sort of creepy. If you was the drinking kind I'd say you'd been hitting up the red-eye."

"The next evening," continued Mary steadily, "I came about dark on a camp-fire with a bed of twigs near it. I stayed by the fire, but no one appeared. Once I thought I heard a horse whinny far away, and once I thought that I saw a streak of white disappear over the top of a hill."

The boy sprang up, shuddering with panic.

"You saw what?"

"Nothing. I thought for a minute that it was a bit of something white, but it was gone all at once."

"White—vanished at once—went into the dark as fast as a horse can gallop?"

"Something like that. Do you think it was someone?"

For answer the boy whipped out his revolver, examined it, and spun the cylinder with shaking hands. Then he said through set teeth: "So you come up here trailin' *him* after you, eh?"

"Who?"

"McGurk!"

The name came like a rifle shot and Mary rose in turn and shrank back toward the wall, for there was murder in the lighted black eyes which stared after her and crumbling fear in her own heart at the thought of McGurk hovering near—of the peril that impended for Pierre. Of the nights in the valley of the Crow she refused to let herself think. Cold beads of perspiration stood out on her forehead.

"You fool—you fool! Damn your pretty pink-and-white face—you've done for us all! Get out!"

Mary moved readily enough toward the door, her teeth chattering with terror in the face of this fury.

Jack continued wildly: "Done for us all; got us all as good as under the sod. I wish you was in— Get out quick, or I'll forget—you're a woman!"

163

He broke into hysterical laughter, which stopped short and finished in a heartbroken whisper: "Pierre!"

30

At that Mary, who stood with her hand on the latch, whirled and stood wide-eyed, her astonishment greater than her fear, for that whisper told her a thousand things.

Through her mind all the time that she stayed in the cabin there had passed a curious surmise that this very place might be the covert of Pierre le Rouge. There was a fatality about it, for the invisible Power which had led her up the valley of the Old Crow surely would not make mistakes.

In her search for Pierre, Providence brought her to this place, and Providence could not be wrong. This, a vague emotion stirring in her somewhere between reason and the heart, grew to an almost certain knowledge as she heard the whisper, the faint, heartbroken whisper: "Pierre!"

And when she turned to the boy again, noting the shirts and the chaps hanging at the wall, she knew they belonged to Pierre as surely as if she had seen him hang them there.

The fingers of Jack were twisted around the butt of his revolver, white with the intensity of the pressure.

Now he cried: "Get out! You've done your work; get out!"

But Mary stepped straight toward the murderous, pale face.

"I'll stay," she said, "and wait for Pierre."

The boy blanched.

"Stay?" he echoed.

The heart of Mary went out to this trusted companion who feared for his friend.

She said gently: "Listen; I've come all this way looking for Pierre, but not to harm him or to betray him, I'm his friend. Can't you trust me Jack?"

"Trust you? No more than I'll trust what came with you!"

And the fierce black eyes lingered on Mary and then fled past her toward the door, as if the boy debated hotly and silently whether or not it would be better to put an end to this intruder, but stayed his hand, fearing that Power which had followed her up the valley of the Old Crow.

It was that same invisible guardian who made Mary strong now; it was like the hand of a friend on her shoulder, like the voice of a friend whispering reassuring words at her ear. She faced those blazing, black eyes steadily. It would be better to be frank, wholly frank.

"This is the house of Pierre. I know it as surely as if I saw him sitting here now. You can't deceive me. And I'll stay. I'll even tell you why. Once he said that he loved me, Jack, but he left me because of a strange superstition; and so I've followed to tell him that I want to be near no matter what fate hangs over him."

And the boy, whiter still, and whiter, looked at her with clearing, narrowing eyes.

"So you're one of them," said the boy softly; "you're one of the fools who listen to Red Pierre. Well, I know you; I've known you from the minute I seen you crouched there at the fire. You're the one Pierre met at the dance at the Crittenden schoolhouse. Tell me!"

"Yes," said Mary, marveling greatly.

"And he told you he loved you?"

"Yes."

It was a fainter voice now, and the color was going up her cheeks.

The lad fixed her with his cold scorn and then turned on his heel and slipped into an easy position on the bunk.

"Then wait for him to come. He'll be here before morning."

But Mary followed across the room and touched the shoulder of Jack. It was as if she touched a wild wolf, for the lad whirled and struck her hand away in an outburst of silent fury.

"Why shouldn't I stay? He hasn't—he hasn't changed—Jack?"

The insolent black eyes looked up and scanned her slowly from head to foot. Then he laughed in the same deliberate manner.

"No, I guess he thinks as much of you now as he ever did."

"You are lying to me," said the girl faintly, but the terror in her eyes said another thing.

"He thinks as much of you as he ever did. He thinks as much of you as he does of the rest of the soft-handed, pretty-faced fools who listen to him and believe him. I suppose—"

He broke off to laugh heartily again, with a jarring, forced note which escaped Mary.

"I suppose that he made love to you one minute and the next told you that bad luck—something about the cross—kept him away from you?"

Each slow word was like a blow of a fist. Mary closed her eyes to shut out the scorn of that handsome, boyish face; closed her eyes to summon out from the dark of her mind the picture of Pierre le Rouge as he had told her of his love; and then she heard the voice of Pierre renouncing her.

She opened her eyes again. She cried:

"It is all a lie! If he is not true, there's no truth in the world."

"If you come down to that," said the boy coldly, "there ain't much wasted this side of the Rockies. It's about as scarce as rain."

He continued in an almost kindly tone: "What would you do with a wild man like Red Pierre? Run along; git out of here; grab your horse, and beat it back to civilization; there ain't no place for you up here in the wilderness."

"What would I do with him?" cried the girl. "Love him!"

It seemed as though her words, like whips, lashed the boy back to his murderous anger. He lay with blazing eyes, watching her for a moment, too moved to speak. At last he propped himself on one elbow, shook a small, white-knuckled fist under the nose of Mary, and cried: "Then what would he do with you?"

He went on: "Would he wear you around his neck like a watch charm?"

"I'd bring him back with me—back into the East, and he would be lost among the crowds and never suspected of his past."

"*You'd* bring Pierre anywhere? Say, lady, that's like hearing the sheep talk about leading the wolf around by the nose. If all the men in the ranges can't catch him, or make him budge an inch out of the way he's picked, do you think you could stir him?"

Jeering laughter shook him; it seemed that he would never be done with his laughter, yet there was a hint of the hysterically mirthless in it. It came to a jarring stop.

He said: "D'you think he's just bein' driven around by chance? Lady, d'you think he even *wants* to get out of this life of his? No, he loves it! He loves the danger. D'you think a man that's used to breathing in a whirlwind can get used to living in calm air? It can't be done!"

And the girl answered steadily: "For every man there is

one woman, and for that woman the man will do strange things."

"You poor, white-faced, whimpering fool," snarled the boy, gripping at his gun again, "d'you dream that *you're* the one that's picked out for Pierre? No, there's another!"

"Another? A woman who—"

"Who loves Pierre—a woman that's fit for him. She can ride like a man; she can shoot almost as straight and as fast as Pierre; she can handle a knife; and she's been through hell for Pierre, and she'll go through it again. She can ride the trail all day with him and finish it less fagged than he is. She can chop down a tree as well as he can, and build a fire better. She can hold up a train with him or rob a bank and slip through a town in the middle of the night and laugh with him about it afterward around a camp-fire. I ask you, is that the sort of a woman that's meant for Pierre?"

And Mary answered, with bowed head: "She is."

She cried instantly afterward, cutting short the look of wild triumph on the face of the boy: "But there's no such woman; there's no one who could do these things! I know it!"

The boy sprang to his feet, flushing as red as the girl was white.

"You fool, if you're blind and got to have your eyes open to see, look at the woman!"

And she tore the wide-brimmed sombrero from her head. Down past the shoulders flooded a mass of blue-black hair. The firelight flickered and danced across the silken shimmer of it. It swept wildly past the waist, a glorious, night-dark tide in which the heart of a strong man could be tangled and lost. With quivering lips Jacqueline cried: "Look at me! Am I worthy of him?"

Short step by step Mary went back, staring with fascinated eyes as one who sees some devilish, midnight revelry, and shrinks away from it lest the sight should blast her.

She covered her eyes with her hands but instantly strong grips fell on her wrists and her hands were jerked down from her face. She looked up into the eyes of a beautiful tigress.

"Answer me—your yellow hair against mine—your child fingers against my grip—are you equal with me?"

But the strength of Jacqueline faded and grew small; her arms fell to her side; she stepped back, with a rising pallor taking the place of the red. For Mary, brushing her hands, one gloved and one bare, before her eyes, returned the stare of the mountain girl with equal scorn. A mighty loathing filled up her veins in place of strength.

"Tell me," she said, "was—was this man living with you when he came to me and—and made speeches—about love?"

"Bah! He was living with me. I tell you, he came back and laughed with me about it, and told me about your baby-blue eyes when they filled with tears; laughed and laughed and laughed, I tell you, as I could laugh now."

The other twisted her hands together, moaning: "And I have followed him, even to the place where he keeps his—woman? Ah, how I hate myself: how I despise myself. I'm unclean—unclean in my own eyes!"

"Wait!" called Jacqueline. "You are leaving too soon. The night is cold."

"I am going. There is no need to gibe at me."

"But wait—he will want to see you! I will tell him that you have been here—that you came clear up the valley of the Old Crow to see him and beg him on your knees to love you—he'll be angry to have missed the scene!"

But the door closed on Mary as she fled with her hands pressed against her ears.

31

Jacqueline ran to the door and threw it open.

"Ride down the valley!" she cried. "That's right. He's coming up, and he'll meet you on the way. He'll be glad—to see you!"

She saw the rider swing sharply about, and the clatter of the galloping hoofs died out up the valley; then she closed the door, dropped the latch, and, running to the middle of the room, threw up her arms and cried out, a wild, shrill yell of triumph like the call of the old Indian brave when he rises with the scalp of his murdered enemy dripping in his hand.

The extended arms she caught back to her breast, and stood there with head tilted back, crushing her delight closer to her heart.

And she whispered: "Pierre! Mine, mine! Pierre!"

Next she went to the steel mirror on the wall and looked long at the flushed, triumphant image. At length she started, like one awakening from a happy dream, and hurriedly coiled the thick, soft tresses about her head. Never before had she lingered so over a toilet, patting each lock into place, twisting her head from side to side like a peacock admiring its image.

Now she looked about hungrily for a touch of color and uttered a little moan of vexation when she saw nothing, till her eyes, piercing through the gloom of a dim corner, saw a spray of autumn leaves, long left there and still stained with beauty. She fastened them at the breast of her shirt, and so arrayed began to cook.

Never was there a merrier cook, not even some jolly French chef with a heart made warm with good red wine, for she sang as she worked, and whenever she had to cross the room it was with a dancing step. Spring was in her blood, warm spring that sets men smiling for no cause except that they are living, and rejoicing with the whole awakening world.

So it was with Jacqueline. Ever and anon as she leaned over the pans and stirred the fire she raised her head and remained a moment motionless, waiting for a sound, yearning to hear, and each time she had to look down again with a sigh.

As it was, he took her by surprise, for he entered with the soft foot of the hunted and remained an instant searching the room with a careful glance. Not that he suspected, not that he had not relaxed his guard and his vigilance the moment he caught sight of the flicker of light through the mass of great boulders, but the lifelong habit of watchfulness remained with him.

Even when he spoke face to face with a man, he never seemed to be giving more than half his attention, for might not someone else approach if he lost himself in order to listen to any one voice? He had covered half the length of the room with that soundless step before she heard, and rose with a glad cry: "Pierre!"

Meeting that calm blue eye, she checked herself mightily.

"A hard ride?" she asked.

"Nothing much."

He took the rock nearest the fire and then raised a glance of inquiry.

"I got cold," she said, "and rolled it over."

He considered her and then the rock, not with suspicion, but as if he held the matter in abeyance for further consideration; a hunted man and a hunter must keep an eye for little things, must carry an armed hand and an armed heart even among friends. As for Jacqueline, her color had risen, and she leaned hurriedly over a pan in which meat was frying.

"Any results?" she asked.

"Some."

She waited, knowing that the story would come at length.

He added after a moment: "Strange how careless some people get to be."

"Yes?" she queried.

"Yes."

Another pause, during which he casually drummed his fingers on his knee. She saw that he must receive more encouragement before he would tell, and she gave it, smiling to herself. Women are old in certain ways of understanding in which men remain children forever.

"I suppose we're still broke, Pierre?"

"Broke? Well, not entirely. I got some results."

"Good."

"As a matter of fact, it was a pretty fair haul. Watch that meat, Jack; I think it's burning."

It was hardly beginning to cook, but she turned it obediently and hid another slow smile. Rising, she passed behind his chair, and pretended to busy herself with something near the wall. This was the environment and attitude which would make him talk most freely, she knew.

"Speaking of careless men," said Pierre, "I could tell you a yarn, Jack."

She stood close behind him and made about his unconscious head a gesture of caress, the overflow of an infinite tenderness.

"I'd sure like to hear it, Pierre."

"Well, it was like this: I knew a fellow who started on the range with a small stock of cattle. He wasn't a very good worker, and he didn't understand cattle any too well, so he didn't prosper for quite a while. Then his affairs took a sudden turn for the better; his herd began to increase. Nobody understood the reason, though a good many suspected, but one man fell onto the reason: our friend was simply running in a few doggies on the side, and he'd arranged a very ingenious way of changing the brands."

"Pierre—"

"Well?"

"What does 'ingenious' mean?"

"Why, I should say it means 'skillful, clever,' and it carries with it the connotation of 'novel.'"

"It carries the con-conno—what's that word, Pierre?"

"I'm going to get some books for you, Jack, and we'll do a bit of reading on the side, shall we?"

"I'd love that!"

He turned and looked up to her sharply.

He said: "Sometimes, Jack, you talk just like a girl."

"Do I? That's queer, isn't it? But go on with the story."

"He changed the brands very skillfully, and no one got the dope on him except this one man I mentioned; and that man kept his face shut. He waited.

"So it went on for a good many years. The herd of our friend grew very rapidly. He sold just enough cattle to keep himself and his wife alive; he was bent on making one big haul, you see. So when his doggies got to the right age and condition for the market, he'd trade them off, one fat doggie for two or three skinny yearlings. But finally he had a really big herd together, and shipped it off to the market on a year when the price was sky-high."

"Like this year?"

"Don't interrupt me, Jack!"

From the shadow behind him she smiled again.

"They went at a corking price, and our friend cleared up a good many thousand—I won't say just how much. He

173

sank part of it in a ruby brooch for his wife, and shoved the rest into a satchel.

"You see how careful he'd been all those years while he was piling up his fortune? Well, he began to get careless the moment he cashed in, which was rather odd. He depended on his fighting power to keep that money safe, but he forgot that while he'd been making a business of rustling doggies and watching cattle markets, other men had been making a business of shooting fast and straight.

"Among others there was the silent man who'd watched and waited for so long. But this silent man hove alongside while our rich friend was bound home in a buckboard.

"'Good evening!' he called.

"The rich chap turned and heard; it all seemed all right, but he'd done a good deal of shady business in his day, and that made him suspicious of the silent man now. So he reached for his gun and got it out just in time to be shot cleanly through the hand.

"The silent man tied up that hand and sympathized with the rich chap; then he took that satchel and divided the paper money into two bundles. One was twice the size of the other, and the silent man took the smaller one. There was only twelve thousand dollars in it. Also, he took the ruby brooch for a friend—and as a sort of keepsake, you know. And he delivered a short lecture to the rich man on the subject of carelessness and rode away. The rich man picked up his gun with his left hand and opened fire, but he'd never learned to shoot very well with that hand, so the silent man came through safe."

"That's a bully story," said Jack. "Who was the silent man?"

"I think you've seen him a few times, at that."

She concealed another smile, and said in the most businesslike manner: "Chow-time, Pierre," and set out the pans on the table.

"By the way," he said easily, "I've got a little present for you, Jack."

And he took out a gold pin flaming with three great rubies.

32

She merely stared, like a child which may either burst into tears or laughter, no one can prophesy which.

He explained, rather worried: "You see, you *are* a girl, Jack, and I remembered that you were pleased about those clothes that you wore to the dance in the Crittenden schoolhouse, and so when I saw that pin I—well—"

"Oh, Pierre!" said a stifled voice. "Oh, Pierre!"

"Jack, you aren't angry, are you? See, when you put it at the throat it doesn't look half bad!"

And to try it, he pinned it on her shirt. She caught both his hands, kissed them again and again, and then buried her face against them as she sobbed. If the heavens had opened and a cloudburst crashed on the roof of the house, he would have been less astounded.

"What is it?" he cried. "Damn it all—Jack—you see—I meant—"

But she tore herself away and flung herself face down on the bunk, sobbing more bitterly than ever. He followed, awestricken—terrified.

He touched her shoulder, but she shrank away and seemed more distressed than ever. It was not the crying of a weak woman: these were heartrending sounds, like the sobbing of a man who has never before known tears.

"Jack—perhaps I've done something wrong—"

He stammered again: "I didn't dream I was hurting you—"

Then light broke upon him.

He said: "It's because you don't want to be treated like a silly girl; eh, Jack?"

But to complete his astonishment she moaned: "N-n-no! It's b-b-because you—you n-n-never *do* t-treat me like a g-g-girl, P-P-Pierre!"

He groaned heartily: "Well, I'll be damned!"

And because he was thoughtful he strode away, staring at the floor. It was then that he saw it, small and crumpled on the floor. He picked it up—a glove of the softest leather. He carried it back to Jacqueline.

"What's this?"

"Wh-wh-what?"

"This glove I found on the floor?"

The sobs decreased at once—broke out more violently— and then she sprang up from the bunk.

"Pierre, I've acted a regular chump. Are you out with me?"

"Not a bit, old-timer. But about this glove?"

"Oh, that's one of mine."

She took it and slipped it into the bosom of her shirt— the calm blue eye of Pierre noted.

He said: "We'll eat and forget the rest of this, if you want, Jack."

"And you ain't mad at me, Pierre?"

"Not a bit."

There was just a trace of coldness in his tone, and she knew perfectly why it was there, but she chose to ascribe it to another cause.

She explained: "You see, a woman is just about nine-tenths fool, Pierre, and has to bust out like that once in a while."

"Oh!" said Pierre, and his eyes wandered past her as though he found food for thought on the wall.

She ventured cautiously, after seeing that he was eating with appetite: "How does the pin look?"

"Why, fine."

And the silence began again.

She dared not question him in that mood, so she ventured again: "The old boy shooting left-handed—didn't he even fan the wind near you?"

"That was another bit of carelessness," said Pierre, but his smile held little of life. "He might have known that if he *had* shot close—by accident—I might have turned around and shot him dead—on purpose. But when a man stops thinking for a minute, he's apt to go on for a long time making a fool of himself."

"Right," she said, brightening as she felt the crisis pass away, "and that reminds me of a story about—"

"By the way, Jack, I'll wager there's a more interesting story than that you could tell me."

"What?"

"About how that glove happened to be on the floor."

"Why, partner, it's just a glove of my own."

"Didn't know you wore gloves with a leather as soft as that."

"No? Well, that story I was speaking about runs something like this—"

And she told him a gay narrative, throwing all her spirit into it, for she was an admirable mimic. He met her spirit more than half-way, laughing gaily; and so they reached the end of the story and the end of the meal at the same time. She cleared away the pans with a few motions and tossed them clattering into a corner. Neat housekeeping was not numbered among the many virtues of Jacqueline.

"Now," said Pierre, leaning back against the wall, "we'll hear about that glove."

"Damn the glove!" broke from her.

"Steady, pal!"

"Pierre, are you going to nag me about a little thing like that?"

"Why, Jack, you're red and white in patches. I'm interested."

He sat up.

"I'm more than interested. The story, Jack."

"Well, I suppose I have to tell you. I did a fool thing today. Took a little gallop down the trail, and on my way back I met a girl sitting in her saddle with her face in her hands, crying her heart out. Poor kid! She'd come up in a hunting party and got separated from the rest.

"So I got sympathetic—"

"About the first time on record that you've been sympathetic with another girl, eh?"

"Shut up, Pierre! And I brought her in here—right into your cabin, without thinking what I was doing, and gave her a cup of coffee. Of course it was a pretty greenhorn trick, but I guess no harm will come of it. The girl thinks it's a prospector's cabin—which it was once. She went on her way, happy, because I told her of the right trail to get back with her gang. That's all there is to it. Are you mad at me for letting anyone come into this place?"

"Mad?" He smiled. "No, I think that's one of the best lies you ever told me, Jack."

Their eyes met, hers very wide, and his keen and steady. Then she gripped at the butt of her gun, an habitual trick when she was very angry, and cried: "Do I have to sit here and let you call me—that? Pierre, pull a few more tricks like that and I'll call for a new deal. Get me?"

She rose, whirled, and threw herself sullenly on her bunk.

"Come back," said Pierre. "You're more scared than angry. Why are you afraid, Jack?"

"It's a lie—I'm not afraid!"

"Let me see that glove again."

"You've seen it once—that's enough."

He whistled carelessly, rolling a cigarette. After he lighted it he said: "Ready to talk yet, partner?"

She maintained an obstinate silence, but that sharp eye saw that she was trembling. He set his teeth and then drew several long puffs on his cigarette.

"I'm going to count to ten, pal, and when I finish you're going to tell me everything straight. In the meantime don't stay there thinking up a new lie. I know you too well, and if you try the same thing on me again—"

"Well?" she snarled, all the tiger coming back in her voice.

"You'll talk, all right. Here goes the count: One—two—three—four—"

As he counted, leaving a long drag of two or three seconds between numbers, there was not a change in the figure of the girl. She still lay with her back turned on him, and the only expressive part that showed was her hand. First it lay limp against her hip, but as the monotonous count proceeded it gathered to a fist.

"Five—six—seven—"

It seemed that he had been counting for hours, his will against her will, the man in him against the woman in her, and during the pauses between the sound of his voice the very air grew charged with waiting. To the girl the wait for every count was like the wait of the doomed traitor when he stands facing the firing-squad, watching the glimmer of light go down the aimed rifles.

For she knew the face of the man who sat there counting; she knew how the firelight flared in the dark red of his hair and made it seem like another fire beneath which the blue of the eyes was strangely cold. Her hand had gathered to a hard-balled fist.

"Eight—nine—"

She sprang up, screaming: "No, no, Pierre!" And threw out her arms to him.

"Ten."

She whispered: "It was the girl with yellow hair—Mary Brown."

33

It was as if she had said: "Good morning!" in the calmest of voices. There was no answer in him, neither word nor expression, and out of ten sharp-eyed men, nine would have passed him by without noting the difference; but the girl knew him as the monk knows his prayers or the Arab his horse, and a solemn, deep despair came over her. She felt like the drowning, when the water closes over their heads for the last time.

He puffed twice again at the cigarette and then flicked the butt into the fire. When he spoke it was only to say: "Did she stay long?"

But his eyes avoided her. She moved a little so as to read his face, but when he turned again and answered her stare she winced.

"Not very long, Pierre."

"Ah," he said. "I see! It was because she didn't dream that this was the place I lived in."

It was the sort of heartless, torturing questioning which was once the cruelest weapon of the inquisition. With all her heart she fought to raise her voice above the whisper whose very sound accused her, but could not. She was condemned to that voice as the man bound in nightmare is condemned to walk slowly, slowly, though the terrible danger is racing toward him, and the safety which he must reach lies only a dozen steps, a dozen mortal steps away.

She said in that voice: "No; of course she didn't dream it."

"And you, Jack, had her interests at heart—her best interests, poor girl, and didn't tell her?"

Her hands went out to him in mute appeal.

"Please, Pierre—don't!"

"Is something troubling you, Jack?"

"You are breaking my heart."

"Why, by no means! Let's sit here calmly and chat about the girl with the yellow hair. To begin with—she's rather pleasant to look at, don't you think?"

"I suppose she is."

"Hm! Rather poor taste not to be sure of it. Well, let it go. You've always had rather queer taste in women, Jack; but, of course, being a long-rider, you haven't seen much of them. At least her name is delightful—Mary Brown! You've no idea how often I've repeated it aloud to myself— Mary Brown!"

"I hate her!"

"You two didn't have a very agreeable time of it? By the way, she must have left in rather a hurry to forget her glove, eh?"

"Yes, she ran—like a coward."

"Ah?"

"Like a trembling coward. How can you care for a white-faced little fool like that? Is she your match? Is she your mate?"

He considered a moment, as though to make sure that he did not exaggerate.

"I love her, Jack, as men love water when they've ridden all day over hot sand without a drop on their lips—you know when the tongue gets thick and the mouth fills with cotton—and then you see clear, bright water, and taste it?

"She is like that to me. She feeds every sense; and when I look in her eyes, Jack, I feel like the starved man on the desert, as I was saying, drinking that priceless water. You knew something of the way I feel, Jack. Isn't it a little odd that you didn't keep her here?"

She had stood literally shuddering during this speech, and now she burst out, far beyond all control: "Because she loathes you; because she hates herself for ever having loved you; because she despises herself for having ridden up here after you. Does that fill your cup of water, Pierre, eh?"

His forehead was shining with sweat, but he set his teeth, and, after a moment, he was able to say in the same hard, calm voice: "I suppose there was no real reason for her change. She can be persuaded back to me in a moment. In that case just tell me where she has gone and I'll ride after her."

He made as if to rise, but she cried in a panic, and yet with a wild exultation: "No, she's done with you forever, and the more you make love to her now the more she'll hate you. Because she knows that when you kissed her before—when you kissed her—you were living with a woman."

"I—living with a woman?"

Her voice had risen out of the whisper for the outbreak. Now it sank back into it.

"Yes—with me!"

"With you? I see. Naturally it must have gone hard with her—Mary! And she wouldn't see reason even when you explained that you and I are like brothers?"

He leaned a little toward her and just a shade of emotion came in his voice.

"When you carefully explained, Jack, with all the eloquence you could command, that you and I have ridden and fought and camped together like brothers for six years? And how I gave you your first gun? And how I've stayed between you and danger a thousand times? And how I've never treated you otherwise than as a man? And how I've given you the love of a blood-brother to take the place of the brother who died? And how I've kept you in a clean and pure respect such as a man can only give once in his life—and then only to his dearest friend? She wouldn't listen—even when you talked to her like this?"

"For God's sake—Pierre!"

"Ah, but you talked well enough to pave the way for me. You talked so eloquently that with a little more persuasion from me she will know and understand. Come, I must be gone after her. Which way did she ride—up or down the valley?"

"You could talk to her forever and she'd never listen. Pierre, I told her that I was—your woman—that you'd told me of your scenes with her—and that we'd laughed at them together."

She covered her eyes and crouched, waiting for the wrath that would fall on her, but he only smiled bitterly on the bowed head, saying: "Why have I waited so long to hear you say what I knew already? I suppose because I wouldn't believe until I heard the whole abominable truth from your own lips. Jack, why did you do it?"

"Won't you see? Because I've loved you always, Pierre!"

"Love—you—your tiger-heart? No, but you were like a cruel, selfish child. You were jealous because you didn't want the toy taken away. I knew it. I knew that even if I rode after her it would be hopeless. Oh, God, how terribly you've hurt me, partner!"

It wrung a little moan from her. He said after a moment: "It's only the ghost of a chance, but I'll have to take it. Tell me which way she rode? No? Then I'll try to find her."

She leaped between him and the door, flinging her shoulders against it with a crash and standing with outspread arms to bar the way.

"You must not go!"

He turned his head somewhat.

"Don't stand in front of me, Jack. You know I'll do what I say, and just now it's a bit hard for me to face you."

"Pierre, I feel as if there were a hand squeezing my heart small, and small, and small. Pierre, I'd die for you!"

"I know you would. I know you would, partner. It was only a mistake, and you acted the way any cold-hearted boy would act if—if someone were to try to steal his horse, for instance. But just now it's hard for me to look at you and be calm."

"Don't try to be! Swear at me—curse—rave—beat me; I'd be glad of the blows, Pierre. I'd hold out my arms to 'em. But don't go out that door!"

"Why?"

"Because—if you found her—she's not alone."

"Say that slowly. I don't understand. She's not alone?"

"I'll try to tell you from the first. She started out for you with Dick Wilbur for a guide."

"Good old Dick, God bless him! I'll fill all his pockets with gold for that; and he loves her, you know."

"You'll never see Dick Wilbur again. On the first night they camped she missed him when he went for water. She went down after a while and saw the mark of his body on the sand. He never appeared again."

"Who was it?"

"Listen. The next morning she woke up and found that

someone had taken care of the fire while she slept, and her pack was lashed on one of the saddles. She rode on that day and came at night to a camp-fire with a bed of boughs near it and no one in sight. She took that camp for herself and no one showed up.

"Don't you see? Someone was following her up the valley and taking care of the poor baby on the way. Someone who was afraid to let himself be seen. Perhaps it was the man who killed Dick Wilbur without a sound there beside the river; perhaps as Dick died he told the man who killed him about the lonely girl and this other man was white enough to help Mary.

"But all Mary ever saw of him was that second night when she thought she saw a streak of white, traveling like a galloping horse, that disappeared over a hill and into the trees—"

"A streak of white—"

"Yes, yes! The white horse—McGurk!"

"McGurk!" repeated Pierre stupidly; then: "And you knew she would be going out to him when she left this house?"

"I knew—Pierre—don't look at me like that—I knew that it would be murder to let you cross with McGurk. You're the last of seven—he's a devil—no man—"

"And you let her go out into the night—to him."

She clung to a last thread of hope: "If you met him and killed him with the luck of the cross it would bring equal bad luck on someone you love—on the girl, Pierre!"

He was merely repeating stupidly: "You let her go out— to him—in the night! She's in his arms now—you devil— you tiger—"

She threw herself down and clung about his knees with hysterical strength.

He tore the little cross from his neck and flung it into her upturned face.

"Don't make me put my hands on you, Jack. Let me go!"

There was no need to tear her grasp away. She crumpled and slipped sidewise to the floor. He leaned over and shook her violently by the shoulder.

"Which way did she ride? Which way did they ride?"

She whispered: "Down the valley, Pierre; down the valley; I swear they rode that way."

And as she lay in a half swoon she heard the faint clatter of galloping hoofs over the rocks and a wild voice yelling, fainter and fainter with distance: "McGurk!"

34

It came back to her like a threat; it beat at her ears and roused her, that continually diminishing cry: "McGurk!" It went down the valley, and Mary Brown, and McGurk with her, perhaps, had gone up the gorge, but it would be a matter of a short time before Pierre le Rouge discovered that there was no camp-fire to be sighted in the lower valley and whirled to storm back up the canyon with that battle-cry: "McGurk!" still on his lips.

And if the two met she knew the result. Seven strong men had ridden together, fought together, and one by one they had fallen, disappeared like the white smoke of the camp-fire, jerked off into thin air by the wind, until only one remained.

How clearly she could see them all! Bud Mansie, meager, lean, with a shifting eye; Garry Patterson, of the red, good-natured face; Phil Branch, stolid and short and muscled like a giant; Handsome Dick Wilbur on his racing bay;

Black Gandil, with his villainies from the South Seas like an invisible mantle of awe about him; and her father, the stalwart, gray Boone.

All these had gone, and there remained only Pierre le Rouge to follow in the steps of the six who had gone before.

She crawled to the door, feeble in mind and shuddering of body like a runner who has spent his last energy in a long race, and drew it open. The wind blew up the valley from the Old Crow, but no sound came back to her, no calling from Pierre; and over her rose the black pyramid of the western peak of the Twin Bears like a monstrous nose pointing stiffly toward the stars.

She closed the door, dragged herself back to her feet, and stood with her shoulders leaning against the wall. Her weakness was not weariness—it was as if something had been taken from her. She wondered at herself somewhat vaguely. Surely she had never been like this before, with the singular coldness about her heart and the feeling of loss, of infinite loss.

What had she lost? She began to search her mind for an answer. Then she smiled uncertainly, a wan, small smile. It was very clear; what she had lost was all interest in life and all hope for the brave tomorrow. Nothing remained of all those lovely dreams which she had built up by day and night about the figure of Pierre le Rouge. He was gone, and the bright-colored bubble she had blown vanished at once.

She felt a slight pain at her forehead and then remembered the cross which Pierre had thrown into her face. Casting that away he had thrown his faintest chance of victory with it; it would be a slaughter, not a battle, and red-handed McGurk would leave one more foe behind him.

But looking down she found the cross and picked up the

shining bit of metal; it seemed as if she held the greater part of Pierre le Rouge in her hands. She raised the cross to her lips.

When she fastened the cross about her throat it was with no exultation, but like one who places over his heart a last memorial of the dead; a consecration, like the red sign or the white which the crusaders wore on the covers of their shields.

Then she took from her breast the spray of autumn leaves. He had not noticed them, yet perhaps they had helped to make him happy when he came into the cabin that night, so she placed the spray on the table. Next she unpinned the great rubies from her throat and let her eye linger over them for a moment. They were chosen stones, a lure and a challenge at once.

The first thought of what she must do came to Jacqueline then, but not in an overwhelming tide—it was rather a small voice that whispered in her heart.

Last, she took from her bosom the glove of the yellow-haired girl. Compared with her stanch riding gloves, how small was this! Yet, when she tried it, it slipped easily on her hand. This she laid in that little pile, for these were the things which Pierre would wish to find if by some miracle he came back from the battle. The spray, perhaps, he would not understand; and yet he might. She pressed both hands to her breast and drew a long breath, for her heart was breaking. Through her misted eyes she could barely see the shimmer of the cross.

She dropped to her knees, and twisted her hands together in agony. It was prayer. There were no words to it, but it was prayer, a wild appeal for aid.

That aid came in the form of a calm that swept on her like the flood of a clear moonlight over a storm-beaten landscape. The whisper which had come to her before was now a solemn-speaking voice, and she knew what she must do. She could not keep the two men apart, but she might reach McGurk before and strike him down by stealth, by craft, any way to kill that man as terrible as a devil, as invulnerable as a ghost.

This she might do in the heart of the night, and afterward she might have the courage left to tell the girl the truth and then creep off somewhere and let this steady pain burn its way out of her heart.

Once she had reached a decision, it was characteristic that she moved swiftly. Also, there was cause for haste, for by this time Pierre must have discovered that there was no one in the lower reaches of the gorge and would be galloping back with all the speed of the cream-colored mare which even McGurk's white horse could not match.

She ran from the cabin and into the little lean-to behind it where the horses were tethered. There she swung her saddle with expert hands, whipped up the cinch, and pulled it with the strength of a man, mounted, and was off up the gorge.

For the first few minutes she let the long-limbed black race on at full speed, a breathless course, because the beat of the wind in her face raised her courage, gave her a certain impulse which was almost happiness, just as the martyrs rejoiced and held out their hands to the fire that was to consume them; but after the first burst of headlong galloping, she drew down the speed to a hand-canter, and this in turn to a fast trot, for she dared not risk the far-echoed sound of the clattering hoofs over the rock.

And as she rode she saw at last the winking eye of red which she longed for and dreaded. She pulled her black to an instant halt and swung from the saddle, tossing the reins over the head of the horse to keep him standing there.

Yet, after she had made half a dozen hurried paces something forced her to turn and look again at the handsome head of the horse. He stood quite motionless, with his ears pricking after her, and now as she stopped he whinnied softly, hardly louder than the whisper of a man. So she ran back again and threw the reins over the horn of the saddle; he should be free to wander where he chose through the free mountains, but as for her, she knew very certainly now that she would never mount that saddle again, or control that triumphant steed with the touch of her hands on the reins. She put her arms around his neck and drew his head down close.

There was a dignity in that parting, for it was the burning of her bridges behind her. She drew back, the horse followed her a pace, but she raised a silent hand in the night and halted him; a moment later she was lost among the boulders.

It was rather slow work to stalk that camp-fire, for the big boulders cut off the sight of the red eye time and again, and she had to make little, cautious detours before she found it again, but she kept steadily at her work. Once she stopped, her blood running cold, for she thought that she heard a faint voice blown up the canyon on the wind: "McGurk!"

For half a minute she stood frozen, listening, but the sound was not repeated, and she went on again with greater haste. So she came at last in view of a hollow in the side of the gorge. Here there were a few trees, growing in the cove, and here, she knew, there was a small spring of clear water. Many a time she had made a cup of her hands and drunk here.

Now she made out the fire clearly, the trees throwing out great spokes of shadow on all sides, spokes of shadows that wavered and shook with the flare of the small fire beyond them. She dropped to her hands and knees and, parting the dense underbrush, began the last stealthy approach.

35

Up the same course which Jacqueline followed, Mary Brown had fled earlier that night with the triumphant laughter of Jack still ringing in her ears and following her like a remorseless, pointed hand of shame.

There is no power like shame to disarm the spirit. A dog will fight if a man laughs at him; a coward will challenge the devil himself if he is whipped on by scorn; and this proud girl shrank and moaned on the saddle. She had not progressed far enough to hate Pierre. That would come later, but now all her heart had room for was a consuming loathing of herself.

Some of that torture went into the spurs with which she punished the side of the bay, and the tall horse responded with a high-tossed head and a burst of whirlwind speed. The result was finally a stumble over a loose rock that almost flung Mary over the pommel of the saddle and forced her to draw rein.

Having slowed the pace she became aware that she was very tired from the trip of the day, and utterly exhausted by the wild scene with Jacqueline, so that she began to look about for a place where she could stop for even an hour or so and rest her aching body.

Thought of McGurk sent her hand trembling to her holster. Still she knew she must have little to fear from him. He had been kind to her. Why had this scourge of the mountain-desert spared her? Was it to track down Pierre?

It was at this time that she heard the purl and whisper of

running water, a sound dear to the hearts of all travelers. She veered to the left and found the little grove of trees with a thick shrubbery growing between, fed by the water of that diminutive brook. She dismounted and tethered the horses.

By this time she had seen enough of camping out to know how to make herself fairly comfortable, and she set about it methodically, eagerly. It was something to occupy her mind and keep out a little of that burning sense of shame. One picture it could not obliterate, and that was the scene of Jacqueline and Pierre le Rouge laughing together over the love affair with the silly girl of the yellow hair.

That was the meaning, then, of those silences that had come between them? He had been thinking, remembering, careful lest he should forget a single scruple of the whole ludicrous affair. She shuddered, remembering how she had fairly flung herself into his arms.

On that she brooded, after starting the little fire. It was not that she was cold, but the fire, at least, in the heart of the black night, was a friend incapable of human treachery. She had not been there long when the tall bay, Wilbur's horse, stiffened, raised his head, arched his tail, and then whinnied.

She started to her feet, stirred by a thousand fears, and heard, far away, an answering neigh. At once all thought of shame and of Pierre le Rouge vanished from her mind, for she remembered the man who had followed her up the valley of the Old Crow. Perhaps he was coming now out of the night; perhaps she would even see him.

And the excitement grew in her pulse by pulse, as the excitement grows in a man waiting for a friend at a station; he sees first the faint smoke like a cloud on the skyline, and then a black speck beneath the smoke, and next the engine draws up on him with a humming of the rails which grows at length to a thunder.

The heart of Mary Brown beat faster, though she could

not see, but only felt the coming of the stranger.

The only sign she saw was in the horses, which showed an increasing uneasiness. Her own mare now shared the restlessness of the tall bay, and the two were footing it nervously here and there, tugging at the tethers, and tossing up their heads, with many a start, as if they feared and sought to flee from some approaching catastrophe—some vast and preternatural change—some forest fire which came galloping faster than even their fleet limbs could carry them.

Yet all beyond the pale of her camp-fire's light was silence, utter and complete silence. It seemed as if a muscular energy went into the intensity of her listening, but not a sound reached her except a faint whispering of the wind in the dark trees above her.

But at last she knew that the thing was upon her. The horses ceased their prancing and stared in a fixed direction through the thicket of shrubbery; the very wind grew hushed above her; she could feel the new presence as one feels the silence when a door closes and shuts away the sound of the street below.

It came on her with a shock, thrilling, terrible, yet not altogether unpleasant. She rose, her hands clenched at her sides and her eyes abnormally wide as they stared in the same direction as the eyes of the two horses held. Yet for all her preparation she nearly fainted when a voice sounded directly behind her, a pleasantly modulated voice: "Look this way. I am here, in front of the fire."

She turned about and the two horses, quivering, whirled toward that sound.

She stepped back, back until the embers of the fire lay between her and that side of the little clearing. In spite of herself the exclamation escaped her—"McGurk!"

The voice spoke again: "Do not be afraid. You are safe, absolutely."

"What are you?"

"Your friend."

"Is it you who followed me up the valley?"

"Yes."

"Come into the light. I must see you." A faint laughter reached her from the dark.

"I cannot let you do that. If that had been possible I should have come to you before."

"But I feel—I feel almost as if you are a ghost and no man of flesh and blood."

"It is better for you to feel that way about it," said the voice solemnly, "than to know me."

"At least, tell me why you have followed me, why you have cared for me."

"You will hate me if I tell you, and fear me."

"No, whatever you are, trust me. Tell me at least what came to Dick Wilbur?"

"That's easy enough. I met him at the river, a little by surprise, and caught him before he could even shout. Then I took his guns and let him go."

"But he didn't come back to me?"

"No. He knew that I would be there. I might have finished him without giving him a chance to speak, girl, but I'd seen him with you and I was curious. So I found out where you were going and why, and let Wilbur go. I came back and looked at you and found you asleep."

She grew cold at the thought of him leaning over her.

"I watched you a long time, and I suppose I'll remember you always as I saw you then. You were very beautiful with the shadow of your lashes against your cheek—almost as beautiful as you are now as you stand over there, fearing and loathing me. I dared not let you see me, but I decided to take care of you—for a while."

"And now?"

"I have come to say farewell to you."

"Let me see you once before you go."

"No! You see, I fear you even more than you fear me."

"Then I'll follow you."

"It would be useless—utterly useless. There are ways of becoming invisible in the mountains. But before I go, tell me one thing: Have you left the cabin to search for Pierre le Rouge in another place?"

"No. I do not search for him."

There was an instant of pause. Then the voice said sharply: "Did Wilbur lie to me?"

"No. I started up the valley to find him."

"But you've given him up?"

"I hate him—I hate him as much as I loathe myself for ever condescending to follow him."

She heard a quick breath drawn in the dark, and then a murmur: "I am free, then, to hunt him down!"

"Why?"

"Listen: I had given him up for your sake; I gave him up when I stood beside you that first night and watched you trembling with the cold in your sleep. It was a weak thing for me to do, but since I saw you, Mary, I am not as strong as I once was."

"Now you go back on his trail? It is death for Pierre?"

"You say you hate him?"

"Ah, but as deeply as that?" she questioned herself.

"It may not be death for Pierre. I have ridden the ranges many years and met them all in time, but never one like him. Listen: six years ago I met him first and then he wounded me—the first time any man has touched me. And afterward I was afraid, Mary, for the first time in my life, for the charm was broken. For six years I could not return, but now I am at his heels. Six are gone; he will be the last to go."

"What are you?" she cried. "Some bloodhound reincarnated?"

He said: "That is the mildest name I have ever been called."

195

36

"Give up the trail of Pierre."

And there, brought face to face with the mortal question, even her fear burned low in her, and once more she remembered the youth who would not leave her in the snow, but held her in his arms with the strange cross above them.

She said simply: "I still love him."

A faint glimmer came to her through the dark and she could see deeper into the shrubbery, for now the moon stood up on the top of the great peak above them and flung a faint light into the hollow. That glimmer she saw, but no face of a man.

And then the silence held; every second of it was more than a hundred spoken words.

Then the calm voice said: "I cannot give him up."

"For the sake of God!"

"God and I have been strangers for a good many years."

"For my sake."

"But you see, I have been lying to myself. I told myself that I was coming merely to see you once—for the last time. But after I saw you I had to speak, and now that I have spoken it is hard to leave you, and now that I am with you I cannot give you up to Pierre le Rouge."

She cried: "What will you have of me?"

He answered with a ring of melancholy: "Friendship? No, I can't take those white hands—mine are so red. All I can do is to lurk about you like a shadow—a shadow with a sting that strikes down all other men who come near you."

She said: "For all men have told me about you, I know you could not do that."

"Mary, I tell you there are things about me, and possibilities, about which I don't dare to question myself."

"You have guarded me like a brother. Be one to me still; I have never needed one so deeply!"

"A brother? Mary, if your eyes were less blue or your hair less golden I might be; but you are too beautiful to be only that to me."

"Listen to me—"

But she stopped in the midst of her speech, because a white head loomed beside the dim form. It was the head of a horse, with pricking ears, which now nosed the shoulder of its master, and she saw the firelight glimmering in the great eyes.

"Your horse," she said in a trembling voice, "loves you and trusts you."

"It is the only thing which has not feared me. When it was a colt it came out of the herd and nosed my hand. It is the only thing which has not fought me, as all men have done—as you are doing now, Mary."

The wind that blew up the gorge came in gusts, not any steady current, but fitful rushes of air, and on one of these brief blasts it seemed to Mary that she caught the sound of a voice blown to whistling murmur. It was a vague thing of which she could not be sure, as faint as a thought. Yet the head of the white horse disappeared, and the glimmer of the man's face went out.

She called: "Whatever you are, wait! Let me speak!"

But no answer came, and she knew that the form was gone forever.

She cried again: "Who's there?"

"It is I," said a voice at her elbow, and she turned to look into the dark eyes of Jacqueline.

"So he's gone?" asked Jack bitterly.

She fingered the butt of her gun.

"I thought—well, my chance at him is gone."

"But what—"

"Bah, if you knew you'd die of fear. Listen to what I have to say. All the things I told you in the cabin were lies."

"Lies?" said Mary evenly. "No, they proved themselves."

"Be still till I've finished, because if you talk you may make me forget—"

The gesture which finished the sentence was so eloquent of hate that Mary shrank away and put the embers of the fire between them.

"I tell you, it was all a lie, and Pierre le Rouge has never loved anything but you, you milk-faced—"

She stopped again, fighting against her passion. The pride of Mary held her stiff and straight, though her voice shook.

"Has he sent you after me with mockery?"

"No, he's given up the hope of you."

"The hope?"

"Don't you see? Are you going to make me crawl to explain? It always seemed to me that God meant Pierre for me. It always seemed to me that a girl like me was what he needed. But Pierre had never seen it. Maybe, if my hair was yellow an' my eyes blue, he might have felt different; but the way it is, he's always treated me like a kid brother—"

"And lived with you?" said the other sternly.

"Like two men! D'you understand how a woman could be the bunky of a man an' yet be no more to him than—than a man would be. You don't? Neither do I, but that's what I've been to Pierre le Rouge. What's that?"

She lifted her head and stood poised as if for flight. Once more the vague sound blew up to them upon the wind. Mary ran to her and grasped both of her hands in her own.

"If it's true—"

But Jack snatched her hands away and looked on the other with a mighty hatred and a mightier contempt.

"True? Why, it damn near finished Pierre with me to think he'd take up with—a thing like you. But it's true. If somebody else had told me I'd of laughed at 'em. But it's true. Tell me: what'll you do with him?"

"Take him back—if I can reach him—take him back to the East."

"Yes—maybe he'd be happy there. But when the spring comes to the city, Mary, wait till the wind blows in the night and the rain comes tappin' on the roof. Then hold him if you can. D'ye hear? Hold him if you can!"

"If he cares it will not be hard. Tell me again, if—"

"Shut up. What's that again?"

The sound was closer now and unmistakably something other than the moan of the wind.

Jacqueline turned in great excitement to Mary:

"Did McGurk hear that sound down the gorge?"

"Yes. I think so. And then he—"

"My God!"

"What is it?"

"Pierre, and he's calling for—d'you hear?"

Clear and loud, though from a great distance, the wind carried up the sound and the echo preserved it: "McGurk!"

"McGurk!" repeated Mary.

"Yes! And you brought him up here with you, and brought his death to Pierre. What'll you do to save him now? Pierre!"

She turned and fled out among the trees, and after her ran Mary, calling, like the other: "Pierre!"

37

After that call first reached him, clear to his ears though vague as a murmur at the ear of Mary, McGurk swung to the saddle of his white horse, and galloped down the gorge like a veritable angel of death.

The end was very near, he felt, yet the chances were at least ten to one that he would miss Pierre in the throat of the gorge, for among the great boulders, tall as houses, which littered it, a thousand men might have passed and repassed and never seen each other. Only the calling of Pierre could guide him surely.

The calling had ceased for some moments, and he began to fear that he had overrun his mark and missed Pierre in the heart of the pass, when, as he rounded a mighty boulder, the shout ran ringing in his very ears: "McGurk!" and a horseman swung into view.

"Here!" he called in answer, and stood with his right hand lifted, bringing his horse to a sharp halt, like some ancient cavalier stopping in the middle of the battle to exchange greetings with a friendly foe.

The other rider whirled alongside, his sombrero's brim flaring back from his forehead, so that McGurk caught the glare of the eyes beneath the shadow.

"So for the third time, my friend—" said McGurk.

"Which is the fatal one," answered Pierre. "How will you die, McGurk? On foot or on horseback?"

"On the ground, Pierre, for my horse might stir and make my work messy. I love a neat job, you know."

"Good."

They swung from the saddles and stood facing each other.

"Begin!" commanded McGurk. "I've no time to waste."

"I've very little time to look at the living McGurk. Let me look my fill before the end."

"Then look, and be done. I've a lady coming to meet me."

The other grew marvelously calm.

"She is with you, McGurk?"

"My dear Pierre, I've been with her ever since she started up the Old Crow."

"It will be easier to forget her. Are you ready?"

"So soon? Come, man, there's much for us to say. Many old times to chat over."

"I only wonder," said Pierre, "how one death can pay back what you've done. Think of it! I've actually run away from you and hidden myself among the hills. I've feared you, McGurk!"

He said it with a deep astonishment, as a grown man will speak of the way he feared darkness when he was a child. McGurk moistened his white lips. The white horse pawed the rocks as though impatient to be gone.

"Listen," said Pierre, "your horse grows restive. Suppose we stand here—it's a convenient distance apart—and wait with our arms folded for the next time the white horse paws the rocks, because when I kill you, McGurk, I want you to die knowing that another man was faster on the draw and straighter with his bullets than you are. D'you see?"

He could not have spoken with a more formal politeness if he had been asking the other to pass first through the door of a dining-room. The wonder of McGurk grew and the sweat on his forehead seemed to be spreading a chill through his entire body.

He said: "I see. You trust all to the cross, eh, Pierre? The little cross under your neck?"

"It's gone," said Pierre le Rouge. "Why should I use it against a night rider, McGurk? Are you ready?"

And McGurk, not trusting his voice for some strange reason, nodded. The two folded their arms.

But the white horse which had been pawing the stones only a moment before was now unusually quiet. The very postures of the men seemed to turn him to stone, a beautiful, marble statue with the moonlight glistening on the muscles of his perfect shoulders.

At length he stirred. At once a quiver jerked through the tense bodies of the waiting men, but the white horse had merely stiffened and raised his head high. Now, with arched neck and flaunting tail he neighed loudly, as if he asked a question. How could he know, dumb brute, that what he asked only death could answer?

And as they waited an itching came at the palm of McGurk's hand. It was not much, just a tingle of the blood. To ease it, he closed his fingers and found that his hand was moist with cold perspiration.

He began to wonder if his fingers would be slippery on the butt of the gun. Then he tried covertly to dry them against his shirt. But he ceased this again, knowing that he must be of hair-trigger alertness to watch for the stamp of the white horse.

It occurred to him, also, that he was standing on a loose stone which might wobble when he pulled his gun, and he cursed himself silently for his hasty folly. Pierre, doubtless, had noticed that stone, and therefore he had made the suggestion that they stand where they were. Otherwise, how could there be that singular calm in the steady eyes which looked across at him?

Also, how explain the hunger of that stare? Was not he McGurk, and was not this man whom he had already once shot down? God, what a fool he had been not to linger an instant longer in that saloon in the old days and place the final shot in the prostrate body! In all his life he had made only one such mistake, and now that folly was pursuing him. And now—

The foot of the white horse lifted—struck the rock. The sound of its fall was lost in the explosion of two guns, and a ring of metal on metal. The revolver snapped from the hand of McGurk, whirled in a flashing circle, and clanged on the rocks at his feet. The bullet of Pierre had struck the barrel and knocked it cleanly from his hand.

It was luck, only luck, that placed that shot, and his own bullet, which had started first, had traveled wild, for there stood Pierre le Rouge, smiling faintly, alert, calm. For the first time in his life McGurk had missed. He set his teeth and waited for death.

But that steady voice of Pierre said: "To shoot you would be a pleasure, but there wouldn't be any lasting satisfaction in it. So there lies your gun at your feet. Well, here lies mine."

He dropped his own weapon to a position corresponding with that of McGurk's.

"We were both very wild that time. We must do better now. We'll stoop for our guns, McGurk. The signal? No, we won't wait for the horse to stamp. The signal will be when you stoop for your gun. You shall have every advantage, you see? Start for that gun, McGurk, when you're ready for the end."

The hand of McGurk stretched out and his arm stiffened but it seemed as though all the muscles of his back had grown stiff. He could not bend. It was strange. It was both ludicrous and incomprehensible. Perhaps he had grown stiff with cold in that position.

But he heard the voice of Pierre explaining gently: "You can't move, my friend. I understand. It's fear that stiffened your back. It's fear that sends the chill up and down your blood. It's fear that makes you think back to your murders, one by one. McGurk, you're done for. You're through. You're ready for the discard. I'm not going to kill you. I've thought of a finer hell than death, and that is to live as you shall live. I've beaten you, McGurk, beaten you fairly on the draw, and I've broken your heart by doing it. The next time you face a man you'll begin to think—you'll begin to remember how one other man beat you at the draw. And that wonder, McGurk, will make your hand freeze to your side, as you've made the hands of other men before me freeze. D'you understand?"

The lips of McGurk parted. The whisper of his dry panting reached Pierre, and the devil in him smiled.

"In six weeks, McGurk, you'll be finished. Now get out!"

And pace by pace McGurk drew back, with his face still toward Pierre.

The latter cried: "Wait. Are you going to leave your gun?"

Only the steady retreat continued.

"And go unarmed through the mountains? What will men say when they see McGurk with an empty holster?"

But the outlaw had passed out of view beyond the corner of one of the monster boulders. After him went the white horse, slowly, picking his steps, as if he were treading on dangerous and unknown ground and would not trust his leader. Pierre was left to the loneliness of the gorge.

The moonlight only served to make more visible its rocky nakedness, and like that nakedness was the life of Pierre under his hopeless inward eye. Over him loomed from either side the gleaming pinnacles of the Twin Bears, and he remembered many a time when he had looked up toward them from the crests of lesser mountains—looked up toward them as a man looks to a great and unattainable ideal.

Here he was come to the crest of all the ranges; here he was come to the height and limit of his life, and what had he attained? Only a cruel, cold isolation. It had been a steep ascent; the declivity of the farther side led him down to a steep and certain ruin and the dark night below. But he stiffened suddenly and threw his head high as if he faced his fate; and behind him the cream-colored mare raised her head with a toss and whinnied softly.

It seemed to him that he had heard something calling, for the sound was lost against the sweep of wind coming up the gorge. Something calling there in the night of the mountains as he himself had called when he rode so wildly in the quest for McGurk. How long ago had that been?

But it came once more, clear beyond all doubt. He recognized the voice in spite of the panting which shook it; a wild wail like that of a heartbroken child, coming closer to him like someone running: "Pierre! Oh, Pierre!"

And all at once he knew that the moon was broad and bright and fair, and the heavens clear and shining with gold points of light. Once more the cry. He raised his arms and waited.

38

So Mary, running through the wilderness of boulders, was guided straight and found Pierre, and before the morning came, they were journeying east side by side, east and down to the cities and a new life; but Jacqueline, a thousand times quicker of foot and surer of eye and ear, missed her goal, went past it, and still on and on, running finally at a steady trot.

Until at last she knew that she had far overstepped her mark and sank down against one of the rocks to rest and think out what next she must do. There seemed nothing left. Even the sound of a gun fired she might not hear, for that sharp call would not travel far against the wind.

It was while she sat there, burying Pierre in her thoughts, a white shape came glimmering down to her through the moonlight. She was on her feet at once, alert and gun in hand. It could only be one horse, only one rider, McGurk coming down from his last killing with the sneer on his pale lips. Well, he would complete his work this night and kill her fighting face to face.

A man's death; that was all she craved. She rose; she stepped boldly out into the center of the trail between the the rocks.

There she saw the greatest wonder she had ever looked on. It was McGurk walking with bare, bowed head, and after him, like a dog after the master, followed the white horse. She shoved the revolver back into the holster. This should be a fair fight.

"McGurk!"

Very slowly the head went up and back, and there he stood, not ten paces from her, with the white moon full on his face. The sneer was still there; the eyelid fluttered in scornful derision. And the heart of Jacqueline came thundering in her throat.

But she cried in a strong voice: "McGurk, d'you know me?"

He did not answer.

"You murderer, you night rider! Look again: it's the last of the Boones!"

The sneer, it seemed to her, grew bitterer, but still the

man did not speak. Then the thought of Pierre, lying dead somewhere among the rocks, burned across her mind. Her hand leaped for the revolver, and whipped it out in a blinding flash to cover him, but with her finger curling on the trigger she checked herself in the nick of time. McGurk had made no move to protect himself.

A strange feeling came to her that perhaps the man would not war against women; the case of Mary was almost proof enough of that. But as she stepped forward, wondering, she looked at the holster at his side and saw that it was empty. Then she understood.

Understood in a daze that Pierre had met the man and conquered him and sent him out through the mountains disarmed. The white horse raised his head and whinnied, and the sound gave a thought to her. She could not kill this man, unarmed as he was; she could do a more shameful thing.

"The bluff you ran was a strong one, McGurk," she said bitterly, "and you had these parts pretty well at a standstill; but Pierre was a bit too much for you, eh?"

The white face had not altered, and still it did not change, but the sneer was turned steadily on her.

She cried: "Go on! Go on down the gorge!"

Like an automaton the man stepped forward, and after him paced the white horse. She stepped between, caught the reins, and swung up to the saddle, and sat there, controlling between her stirrups the best-known mount in all the mountain-desert. A thrill of wild exultation came to her. She cried: "Look back, McGurk! Your gun is gone, your horse is gone; you're weaker than a woman in the mountains!"

Yet he went on without turning, not with the hurried step of a coward, but still as one stunned. Then, sitting quietly in the saddle, she forgot McGurk and remembered Pierre. He was happy by this time with the girl of the yellow hair; there was nothing remaining to her from him except the ominous cross which touched cold against her breast. That he had abandoned as he had abandoned her.

What, then, was left for her? The horse of an outlaw for her to ride; the heart of an outlaw in her breast.

She touched the white horse with the spurs and went at a reckless gallop, weaving back and forth among the boulders down the forge. For she was riding away from the past.

The dawn came as she trotted out into a widening valley of the Old Crow. To maintain even that pace she had to use the spurs continually, for the white horse was deadly weary, and his head fell more and more. She decided to make a brief halt, at last, and in order to make a fire that would take the chill of the cold morning from her, she swung up to the edge of the woods. There, before she could dismount, she saw a man turn the shoulder of the slope. She drew the horse back deeper among the trees and waited.

He came with a halting step, reeling now and again, a big man, hatless, coatless, apparently at the last verge of exhaustion. Now his foot apparently struck a small rock, and he pitched to his face. It required a long struggle before he could regain his feet; and now he continued his journey at the same gait, only more uncertainly than ever, close and closer. There was something familiar now about the fellow's size, and something in the turn of his head. Suddenly she rode out, crying: "Wilbur!"

He swerved, saw the white horse, threw up his hands high above his head, and went backward, reeling, with a hoarse scream which Jacqueline would never forget. She galloped to him and swung to the ground.

"It's me—Jack. D'you hear?"

He would not lower those arms, and his eyes stared

wildly at her. On his forehead the blood had caked over a cut; his shirt was torn to rags, and the hair matted over his eyes. She caught his hands and pulled them down.

"It's not McGurk! Don't you hear me? It's Jack!"

He reached out, like a blind man who has to see by the sense of touch, and stroked her face.

"Jack!" he whispered at last. "Thank God!"

"What's happened?"

"McGurk—"

A violent palsy shook him, and he could not go on.

"I know—I understand. He took your guns and left you to wander in this hell! Damn him! I wish—"

She stopped.

"How long since you've eaten?"

"Years!"

"We'll eat—McGurk's food!"

But she had to assist him up the slope to the trees, and there she left him propped against a trunk, his arms fallen weakly at his sides, while she built the fire and cooked the food. Afterward she could hardly eat, watching him devour what she placed before him; and it thrilled all the woman in her to a strange warmth to take care of the long-rider. Then, except for the disfigured face and the bloodshot eyes, he was himself.

"Up there? What happened?"

He pointed up the valley.

"The girl and Pierre. They're together."

"She found him?"

"Yes."

He bowed his head and sighed.

"And the horse, Jack?" He said it with awe.

"I took the horse from McGurk."

"You!"

She nodded. After all, it was not a lie.

"You killed McGurk?"

She said coolly: "I let him go the way he let you, Dick. He's on foot in the mountains without a horse or a gun."

"It isn't possible!"

"There's the horse for proof."

He looked at her as if she were something more than human.

"Our Jack—did this?"

"We've got to start on. Can you walk, Dick?"

"A thousand miles now."

Yet he staggered when he tried to rise, and she made him climb up to the saddle. The white horse walked on, and she kept her place close at the stirrup of the rider. He would have stopped and dismounted for her a hundred times, but she made him keep his place.

"What's ahead of us, Jack? We're the last of the gang?"

"The last of Boone's gang. We are."

"The old life over again?"

"What else?"

"Yes; what else?"

"Are you afraid, Dick?"

"Not with you for a pal. Seven was too many; with two we can rule the range."

"Partners, Dick?"

How could he tell that her voice was gone so gentle because she was seeing in her mind's eye another face than his? He leaned toward her.

"Why not something more than partners, after a while, Jack?"

She smiled strangely up to him.

"Because of this, Dick."

And fumbling at her throat, she showed him the glittering metal of the cross.

"The cross goes on, but what of you, Jack?"

A long silence fell between them. Words died in the making.

The great weight pressing down on that slender throat was like the iron hand of a giant, but slowly, one by one, the sounds marshalled themselves:

". . . God knows . . ." It was the passing of Judgment. "God knows . . . not I."

Epilogue

But what of the legendary gunfighter, McGurk? How could the spirit of any man survive that terrible defeat at the hands of Red Pierre?

After that night, when he had walked from the dark heart of the mountain without horse or gun, head bowed, eyes glazed, it seemed that the life of Bob McGurk had burned down to black ash.

Indeed, no one heard of him for five long years. Then, phoenix-like, he was reborn in fire, emerging in the raw border country of Texas. His rebirth was spectacular. No longer the lone phantom fighter of past days, he led a gang of coldhearted thieves and killers that became the scourge of the Rio Grande.

But McGurk never returned to the mountain-desert country of his shame and defeat. And only he knew that the face of Red Pierre never left him; it blazed in his mind by day and haunted his nights.

Then, as suddenly as he had reappeared, after proving his skill and courage afresh in a score of wild, bullet-filled encounters, the great gunfighter vanished from the world of civilized men. His gang dispersed and the border country saw no more of him.

McGurk was finally gone.

Only the legend remained.